Work in Progress

A Woman's Point of View

Sonya Lowe

For more information about the Author, please visit

www.sonyalowe.com

RealityWorks Publishing

PO Box 11134

Torrance, CA 90510

www.realityworkspublishing.net

First published by RealityWorks Pub. on 6/14/2009.

Printed in the United States of America.

This book is printed on acid-free paper.

This book is dedicated in loving memory of my father,
a man of honor and true integrity.
I'm praying to go to Heaven so that I can see you again, rest
in peace Daddy…

Albert "A.C." Young
May 14, 1927 ~ September 28, 2001

For Avery & Payton, years from now…
You both will truly understand

My role is to be responsible enough to reveal all things
that represent honesty, loyalty and self-respect by the
example that I set and the way I live my life…

My love for you both is unwavering and unconditional
and my joy comes from being loved by the two of you…

Mommy

Acknowledgements

I could never have it said that I didn't let you know how thankful I am for your prayers, encouragement and support. My old friends and my new friends, as well as my family – I salute you! Thank you for feeling my tears. If I don't specifically mention you, still know that you are an important component in all that is real for me... Thank you Avery and Payton for being precious babies. A special thanks to my mother, Tommie Young, for wanting nothing but the best for me ~ I apologize for the profanity; I know it's not the language of a Lady but sometimes you have to speak in a tongue that they understand... All my people: Galen Babb, Monica Laurent, Deborah Beavers, Pat Dial, Andrea Morgan, Sandra Jenkins, The Young Family ~ Ryan, Ayanna, Royal, DeShawn, Monique, Rodney – the BIG one and the little one, Tysen, Sydnee, Jeremy, Lennard, Tiffeany, Anthony, T-Bone, Kevin, Doreen, Tyra, my e-Sister Circle, Ron Carter, Sincere Honoree, my attorney Jayne Whittaker, my agent & manager, Michael Dunn, Alpha Kappa Alpha Sorority, Border's Bookstores, Limitless, Inc., Amazon.com, Lulu.com and Barnes and Nobles Bookstores nationwide...

Thanks to everyone who had the courage to get involved in this project. I am forever in your debt... Spread love today ~ tomorrow is not promised! You owe it to yourself. Love responsibly...

Karma's Story...

Survival and ways to cope with everyday life has taken center stage in the lives of women around the world. Though I don't believe that survival in Los Angeles is unique, I do believe that Los Angeles offers challenges that are unique from anywhere else in the continental United States and Canada. For instance, I've been trying to tell my side of the story for years with no one to tell it too. No I'm not a video vixen or getting my groove back; I'm actually living day to day with hopes that the Lord will show me the right steps to take (because stepping on my own has proven to be ill-fated in the long run ~ short run too!).

This isn't one of those "sistah get it together and conquer the world" books or even a gripping tale of how some of us overcome the odds, but more so how we have to stay one step ahead of the odds and rob the devil several times to keep our sanity. It's about being a thirty-something divorced woman who hung up her party dress over five years ago to be back out here trying to meet a man – a suitable man (at a time when suitable is breathing without a ventilator). It's about stepping back and laughing at the things that are meant to hurt. My story is not Black or White; rich or poor. It's about being a successful business woman, mother, daughter and woman of strong conviction, but having to always do battle with life's circumstances. Doing everything right to only have everything go wrong...

In the world we live in, self-help really means help yourself. I know because I have a bookcase full of everything from TD Jakes to Patti Labelle's southern cook book. All that to try to get "this" right. You know, find a way to be a perfect woman. But when life is in full affect and you're paying bills, raising kids, running a business, keeping a eye on a sneaky ass man and trying to keep all your plates spinning, it helps to find humor in those things that make you want to cry. I must say that a lot of things hurt me along the way but without rain there would be no sunshine. You will probably see bits and pieces of yourself in some of the shit I go through. My story is just like yours but I decided to start the healing process and have a few things to say – get some shit off my chest...

You see, I'm Karma Bennard Gregory and I'm just like you. Neither you nor I will lose our souls or comprise our values in the search of inner peace and self acceptance.

All I can tell you is what I've experienced. Now I don't know about anyone else but my circumstances lead me to believe that what you do comes back to you – good, bad, and indifferent. If you do someone wrong, simply wait your turn because it will come back to you and threefold. Give it to the universe and the universe gives it back, right? Follow me through circumstances and situations that only confirm that Karma is alive and well and living in Los Angeles.

Chapter One: What Just Happened?

*"Now faith is the assurance of things hoped for, the
conviction of things not seen, for by it the men of old
receive Devine approval"*
Hebrews 11:1-2

It's my fifth wedding anniversary and I'm sitting in Jerry's Deli with my girlfriend, Danica, drinking apple martinis. I lost interest in this "thing called marriage" about three years ago. There has always been something missing and I never really could put my finger on it. You see, I was like a lot of women, rushing to the alter because "it's was time" to be married. I have always taken great pride in simply being me, Karma Bernard, and then all of a sudden, I'm transformed into Karma Gregory, someone I don't even recognize. What a hard transformation it has been.

During our year long courtship I may have cooked dinner a handful of times. Right after we said "I do" and "we will", I'm supposed to magically become Betty Crocker. Lucky me... I went from stilettos to sneakers; from silk to flannel; from lobster to hamburger helper. You heard it from me, this thing they call holy matrimony hasn't been all its cracked up to be, *but it was time*.

I got married five years ago to a man that I thought would be the answer to many of my prayers, so you can imagine the disappointment in realizing that he didn't even believe truly in God. Go figure.

Nonetheless, over the past five years we have managed to have two wonderful little boys and they make all the uncertainty; all the unhappiness; and frankly speaking, all the straight bullshit, worth it. I have blamed myself time and time again for wanting to be married so bad that anyone would do but I have realized that wasn't it all. I wasn't ill-prepared or immature but just the opposite. I already had my undergraduate degree and was working on my doctorate when he and I met. I can't say I didn't have my doubts because I had plenty of them. I mean you can find sex anywhere, so there had to be something more to it. I have always been responsible and level headed; it was my selection process that got me into this mess.

To bring you up to speed, my husband, Adam (my girls and I call him Mister because they tease me about him reminding them of the character in the Color Purple) had a love-hate relationship with his ex-girlfriend. They had a child together when he and I got together. Yeah, this should have been a red flag but did I mention the sex was good? Anyway, for whatever reason she remains fully invested in Mister and all his drama. They had many violent episodes during their relationship; some of which landed him in court ordered domestic violence classes. Whatever the case, she blames me for every problem she has with him because of the lazy notion that the wife is always the enemy. So fuck it, I'll be all that and some more! From whatever lens you peek into this mini-drama, the whole situation has taken a tremendous toll on our marriage. Yes, I knew not to lend energy to a man that had already started a family out of wedlock but I thought maybe our situation would be different. I knew that she would hold on for dear life but I thought he would be different and not bring all the baby mama drama into my life.

Well you can see where I went wrong with that thought process. But the sex was good...

I would never forget to give an honorable mention to his mother (which is equivalent to mother fucker in my book). I had always heard about the mother-in-laws from hell but never thought it would actually happen to me. It did. She is not only emotionally unstable from all the abuse that she had to endure from Mister's father for sixteen years, but she is a shit starter too. She is so full of mess that she smells just like shit! And believe me, the more chaos she brings to the table the happier this bitch is. I have never cared about what she says and does, as long as she says or does it far away from me. Really, I haven't (for real, I haven't).

She and Mister's father had divorced some twelve years ago and she locked herself in her room, away from the outside world, for ten years. The divorce had such a crippling affect on her that all she would do was go to work and come home. That was it. I guess it is understandable because they married as teenagers and maybe it was fashionable to give up all your power to a man who kicked your ass for years. Despite the place she holds in my life, I do find it sad that a woman would value herself so little that she thought she wasn't worthy to go on after leaving a man that she claims was Satan in the flesh. My only question would be this: what in the hell did she do for sex? Was she really fucking herself in that room for all those years? Don't act like you don't know stuff like that happens. If you're in a room for ten years by yourself, you got to be in there fucking something – fruit, bed post, hair spray bottles, something! You never know, that may be the reason she was locked up for so long. I guess it worked for her.

Mister isn't innocent in it all. Matter of fact, I think he gets a true kick out of the constant fire between myself, his mother and his ex-lover. Let's face it, if he didn't like it he would do something to control it. He would stand up and be a man for his family. He would definitely stop telling me to ignore his mother's shit. And me, take the back seat to a project chick and a baby she conceived as a meal ticket, *please*. Get real. If

Mister wasn't getting off to this chaos he would get these two bitches before I do! It hasn't happened over the past five years and I don't have another five to wait to see what'll take place.

"Danica, girl I got to go. I'm supposed to meet Mister for dinner tonight. It is our anniversary you know?"

"Girl, just clear your head and don't go into the fifth year feeling like it won't work. You'd be surprised how many people are able to create a loving relationship after one of them has an affair."

Oh, I failed to mention that Mister had several sexual encounters over the past five years. I mean, I wouldn't call them affairs because to qualify, it would have to be validated by one of the parties involved having some form of passion or even bond with one another. In Mister's case, it was just anyone that would have sex with him. Needless to say, he scrapped the bottom of the barrel to find women with the lowest self esteem which equated to the only type of woman that would waste her time with a married man with three kids and an airplane full of emotional baggage.

On a side note, I always wondered if Mister was a switch hitter but I never asked. I really didn't see the point in adding insult to injury but the point was that there was certainly something in his actions that seemed a little extreme. It appeared he would overstate his manhood to hide his desire for something else. Shit I don't know, I think if I had asked I would have been featured on "Snapped" and where would my children be then?

"I'm out of here Danica. You have a good weekend and keep me in your prayers. Lord knows I will need the strength to make it through this weekend without killing this fool." I say before dashing out the door.

***

My cell phone is ringing off the hook and I know its Mister. *Yes*, I'm late. *Purposely late*. Later than Mister and he holds the record. He has to know that something is brewing because I'm always on time but I really don't want to face him today – not knowing that I have wasted the past five years fucking around with him and all the bullshit that came with him!

"Where are you? I've been waiting here for over an hour. Are you coming or what?" He asks.

Mister has finally lost his mind! I should care that he's been waiting a precious sixty minutes when I have waited five years for his punk ass to arrive! But stop the presses because he's been waiting, I should get excited and rush to make him happy. No such luck! If I can be unhappy for five years, he's due to be unhappy for an hour or two.

"I went to happy hour with Danica and lost track of time but I'm on the 405 freeway right now so I should be there shortly." I said in a patronizing tone.

"I really have something that I want to talk with you about and I would like to talk with you face to face."

"You can talk to me now – I'm alone."

"Well I would rather not do this over the phone." he says.

"Look we're well pass the whole emotional thing so if you have something say, now would be the time to say it."

"Well Karma this just isn't working for me. I'm not happy and you're not happy so why are we kidding ourselves?" He says in quiet voice.

No he didn't just tell me this over the phone! This bitch-made mutha fucka! How insensitive can you be? I have two children with his ass and he's telling me something so heart wrenching over the damn phone! Now, cut to reality as I remind myself that this is my long-awaited escape route.

Who am I kidding? Any chance he gives me to get out of this, I'm running like hell. Trust that. Gladys Knight said it best, "neither one of us wants to be the first to say good bye." Oddly enough I'm relieved that he said it and I didn't have to but something in his voice made me think he was expecting an emotional breakdown or crying or some other unnecessary bullshit but instead it was like a weight lifted off my shoulders. I responded.

"You know, I'm glad you said that because I feel the same way and it is a relief to know you feel the same way too. It has been a long time since I was getting what I needed out of this marriage and I really want to move on and explore deeper areas of myself."

There was a dead silence. He wanted the crying and begging and all that foolishness. Not going to happen. If he just realized it wasn't going to work, then he's three years late. For me, the thrill has *been* gone and I'm looking forward to being free.

"So maybe you can move your things out of the house until we settle things and map out how we will divide things and see where we stand."

"Yeah, I can do that," he said, "but I want you to know that you have a lot of nerves to not even care about what I'm saying and to not even hesitate with your response. Fuck it! You win."

Who's zooming who my brotha? Mister thought I would be devastated but he, his mother and his crazy bitch on the outside have already drained me of any energy I had left to work on a marriage. I've been too busy fighting with these two bitches about matters of my household and without having Mister's backing or support. I have had a full dose of the whole three of them and want to prepare for the future of me and my two sons – ALONE! I had always been alone in the marriage anyway so nothing would change except Mister's ass wouldn't be expecting dinner on Sundays – or at least not from me.

I had been alone in theory for the last three years anyway but now I would be alone for real. *What just happened?*

I have contemplated that conversation to some degree for many, many moons now but I never thought that it would be so concrete and absolute. And I certainly didn't think that he possessed the ability to make something so wonderfully easy on me. Although I had been divorced emotionally for years, it was something about breathing life into it that made it resonate in my mind. The Lord has given me the strength, courage and wisdom to know that the kids and

I deserve so much more and I am faithful that He will walk this journey with me. To be honest, I'm not even expecting it to be a smooth ride, but it damn sure beats traveling by donkey.

One day I hope I will miss something – anything – that Mister brought to my life. Unfortunately, right now I can't think of anything but my life without him. I'm looking forward to being my old self again. *Hello me!*

Chapter Two: Who Is It?

"But we are not of those who shrink back and are destroyed, but of those who have faith and keep their souls"
Hebrews 11:39

At three o'clock in the morning who could be foolish enough to ring someone's phone? It could be important but if it had waited until now, it could surely wait another hour or two. I have to answer it though because it could be an emergency with my father. My parents are getting up in age and I always make it a point to be available to them any time of day or night. Like most people, all of my accomplishments are credited to my parents. You know what they say; when you're a baby your goal is to make your parents smile. I believe that because my father and this whole cancer thing makes me revert back to childhood and all I want to do is freeze his smile in time. It hurts so bad to see him endure this battle. He has fought so many battles for me and now I feel so helpless because there is absolutely nothing that I can do. Lord knows if I could take the pain away, I would. My Daddy is a trooper though and he remains so positive even though everyone around him is scared to death.

Scared to ever know what life would be like without him. I'm terrified! So to answer the phone in the wee hours of the morning is my duty; an obligation to my parents. I say "hello" but the person on the other end doesn't say a word. So I say "hello" again. This time the person speaks. The voice is deep, strong and down right intoxicating. All I could think is that this must be a wrong number and this man is making a "booty call." Do people still use that term, *Booty Call?* What the hell, it is what it is – booty call or whatever – obviously there's been a mistake.

"Hello, Did I wake you?"

I have no idea who the male voice could be but he had to know that anyone who had to work the following day would have to be fast asleep at three in the morning.

"You actually did wake me. You must have the wrong number so I'm going to hang so you can dial the right number, okay?" I reply.

"I'm really hurt that you don't know my voice and maybe I will just hang up and call you back in the morning. You know give you some time to wake up." the voice said.

Can you get ready for that? Wake me up at day break only to say he will call back when I'm awake. How crazy is that. This man is a complete fool. And that stuff about being hurt about me not recognizing his voice had to be a joke in itself. Every since Mister moved out a few months ago, I have made it a point to be by myself so there shouldn't be a man breathing fresh air that can be hurt by anything involving me. Now that's real…

"Look man, I don't know what game you're playing and frankly, I don't care but you need to hang up and do whatever it is you're trying to do. You have a good one, okay?"

"Wait a minute, hold on before you hang up, it's Erik," he says.

I had to think fast; who the hell is Erik? It had to be what I originally thought – a booty call. I don't know anyone name Erik so there's no need for me to waste his time.

"Erik, I'm sorry but you have the wrong number. You have a good morning."

"Is this Karma Gregory?"

Now I'm puzzled. He knows my name and he knows my telephone number. This just could be Mister putting someone up to calling my house to see if I'm horny enough to bite at getting with a man over the phone. He's crazy enough to do something like this and for whatever reason, he's preoccupied with whoever he thinks may be keeping my bed warm. Mister has been full of fun and games every since he realized that I was serious about getting on with my life without his ass. It's like this; Mister has learned the value of water now...

"Look Erik, yes this *is* Karma and I don't know what game you're playing but I'm not for it so I do hope that you hang up this phone and don't call this number anymore. Because I don't have time..."

"Karma, I apologize for calling you this time of morning but I wanted to make sure that this was the right number and so I thought I would reach out to you tonight and really didn't know it was this late – or this early – however you want to look at it."

"What are you doing up this time of morning anyway?"

You really have to ask these days. I'm from the neighborhood and its three o'clock in the morning which makes me a little curious. Nobody's up this time of morning but crack heads and drug dealers, so he just may be one of the two. Or worst, just plain fucking crazy…

More so, I have been bullshit-free for ninety-eight days and counting and I'm not contemplating inviting insanity into my world, space, spirit – none of that. My world is good right now and I'm not even trying to do anything that resembles some crazy shit that will cloud my vision and block my focus. You know what though, I haven't had the number long enough for this man to be some long lost boyfriend; *they all had the old number.*

"I just got back from Atlanta and you said to call you when I made it back, so I'm calling you because I have been thinking about you all while I was gone…" he says.

Did I say that? Wow! I would have said anything to this man if he looks anything like he sounds. I don't want to tell him that I'm clueless but I'm clueless. I have no idea who Erik is and I don't recall any Erik going to Atlanta and damn sure can't figure out why he would be thinking of me while he's there. If, in fact, I met this Erik character I should certainly remember something about him. Normally I'm good at remembering names and faces but I can't place either one. Anyway, I'm still not convinced that this man is not calling my house on some shit Mister fed him but I know it's too damn early to be playing.

> "Erik, I got to be honest with you, I just don't remember who you are so hang up this damn phone and don't call this number again, playing games and interrupting my sleep..."

> "Karma, I never meant to offend you so please accept my apology. We met when your company handled the marketing campaign for

my venture capital investment group. You promised me a rain check on my dinner invitation and its raining last I checked. I hope you would do me the honor of having dinner with me on Thursday evening. Please say yes."

That's certainly some playa shit there – do him the honor of having dinner. And he definitely knows me. Unfortunately for me a lot of things have happened over the last couple of months so I guess I really am on auto pilot. But because he calls me in the wee hours with some smooth shit that actually tickles my ear, I'm suppose to go running off to meet some strange ass man for dinner. I don't think so. No sir, not me. That would be insane, crazy, foolish and just down right out of the question. Did I mention desparate? Anyway, I'm a lady and I'm busy doing me. In all my splendor, by myself. *By my damn self...* I guess it wouldn't hurt to agree to dinner in a public place just to see what this man looks like and maybe get a decent meal and conversation out of the deal. What's wrong with that...

"Normally I would say no but because you had the gall to call me this time of morning, I'm going to say yes but I will have to call you to confirm because I have some pressing issues and – "

"No problem. I understand and I am looking forward to seeing you. Do you have a pen to write down my number?"

He gives me his number and we hang up. Now that was certainly an easy pick up, if I must say myself. I hope he's not some psychotic maniac that's stalking me or that was sent by Mister to brutally rape my fine ass and bludgeon me to death. You think? I wish he would have called at three o'clock in the afternoon rather than morning because the boys will hit the floor in about two hours and at this point, it will take me about an hour and a half to get back to sleep. This man sure better be worth me breaking my sleep. And he'd better hope he looks as good as he sounds because I'm not going to bite my tongue and I'm certainly not having dinner with some old ass man that has to wrap a couple strands of hair around a bald spot. Just my luck, he'll be old, bald, walk with a limp and have a crooked eye. Why the hell did I agree to dinner with this man, sight unseen? That's like buying a used car over the internet. At least with that you know what the make and model looks like. What was I thinking?

Foolish of me, I didn't even get his last name. I could have asked around the office to see who knows the mysterious Erik, who calls me in the wee hours of the morning just to ask me out to dinner. Hell, if I had his last name I could do a criminal background check and find out who he *really* is, you feel me. Whatever the case may be, the boys will hit the floor and we will be back to the hustle and bustle of everyday life so I better get to sleep while I still can.

***

Like clock work, Justin and Kyle hit the floor and start their normal routine – argue for about thirty minutes and then start fighting over who will shower first. I don't understand why they must fight about everything – I mean every single thing. It's sad to say but this has become a way of life in our house since the separation. I'm slowly starting to regain some control over my household; it has been impossible to make calm out of chaos. My boys have suffered somewhat while I find a groove; a rhythm so to speak that works for me. I have started finding out what really makes me happy, especially since I realize that Mister was the root of all evil up in here and definitely the reason for my discontent. I recognize that my children bring me more joy than anything else in the world. I love being with them and hearing their point of view. You can actually learn a lot from a four and five year old. A mature four and five year old, that is.

I'm not one of those mothers who likes to drop the kids off to Grandma for the weekend so that I can go clubbing, chasing men or whatever. I think I did enough clubbing in the nineties to last a lifetime. As for chasing men, I could really care less. Right now I'm in "fuck 'em all" mode so I'm not tripping that shit either. I do remember the good old days though, when I could drink all night long and still make it to work on time and give a full eight hours (minus the hour or so that I sit at my desk dozing off). And as DJ Quik would say, *"turn around and do the same old thang tonight"*. I guess those would be called the good old days for the thirty something crowd. I have a drink now and I'm in the bed for the next three days trying to recover.

The kids are going to be with Mister this weekend and I will be left alone for the next couple of days. I'm starting to like being alone. This peace of mind and not having to cook dinner for anyone's special taste buds is well-deserved. Being alone allows me to explore more about myself. I mean I recently discovered that I like Jazz music. Hip hop has always been my thing; you know your Mary J., Faith Evans, and Notorious B.I.G. – the whole Bad Boy family. All of a sudden Wynton Marsalis and Kem are in my CD player and I love it! I bet you my old crowd would never believe that I even know a Natalie Cole song, let alone have an entire CD. So the good part about this time is that I'm discovering bigger pieces of myself instead of conforming to what everyone around me likes. Being alone is a beautiful thing! Yes it is...

"Mom, do we have to go to Dad's this weekend?" Kyle asks.

"Yes you do." I reply while hastily making lunch for the two of them.

"But why do we have to go? I don't want to go other there. I hate it over there. Why can't we just stay home with you? You don't have anything to do." Kyle pouts.

Now how the hell would this little boy know if I have something to do? I would be mommy dearest if I turned around and told him that he's going his ass to his dad's because I want to be left the fuck alone. How about that! I didn't, but I really could have. Really I could.

"Why don't you want to go is the question Kyle?"

"Because we don't like him very much anymore so we should just stay home with you." Justin chimes in.

"Well it's like this gentlemen, when you don't go and it's his scheduled weekend, your dad thinks it's me trying to keep you away from him. I want you guys to love and respect your father so we all have to compromise."

"Did you know his girlfriend lives with him now?" they say.

"You two need to quit and just know that you're going to your father's house this weekend. I don't owe you an explanation. You're just going. Case closed."

"But Mom, he has us around his stupid girlfriend that he found in the soul food restaurant. You haven't even met her and he knows you won't like her because she's ghetto and hoochie." Justin shouts.

"That's between me and your daddy so eat your breakfast so that you can be on time to school and I can get to work." I say while trying not to let them know just how pissed I really am.

Now he has a hell of a lot of nerves, taking my children around some ghetto whore that he met in a soul food restaurant. He knows he should have introduced me to this bitch before ever having my kids around her. But this bastard can't ever do anything right. If it's not fucked up, he can't function. And to get a bitch out the soul food restaurant after being with me; highly educated with two degrees and a company that nets at least a million dollars of annual profits. He's one crazy mother fucka! But reality is that this woman, ghetto and uneducated, is exactly what Mister needs; he may be able to control her. He damn sure couldn't control me!

My grandmother use to always say that the way to a man's heart is through his stomach and apparently Mister wants heartburn or acid reflux. That whole cooking thing, I just can't get with it. Frankly speaking, all while we were dating Mister only wanted me to cook in the bedroom and soon after we got married, I'm in a smoke filled kitchen. Damn! What's that all about? Well shit with the way Mister eats, he should get all his women from a soul food joint – or taco bell, the waffle hut, the chicken shack, gourmet grits, whatever. I'm going to leave that whole cooking thing to those who want to do domestic shit. The fact is, he has my children around this woman I have never met and he thinks he's slick. Nobody wants some whore they have never met and around her two sons, I don't care how old they are. He really thinks he's slick. A mother fucka!

Now my first mind tells me to call that asshole and give him an earful but you know what? I think I will chill on this one. I'm learning to pick my battles and if she's willing to tolerate my kids every couple of weekends without incident, I can hold my tongue until something happens that gives me no choice but to have to go dead off. Curiosity makes me want to know who this woman is because I know how Mister gets down and I'm just hoping that this woman is not a crack head or a professional ~ you know, *a real professional.*

Chapter Three: What's Really Going On?

*"Judge not, and you will not be judged; condemn not,
and you will not be condemned; forgive, and you will be
forgiven"*
Luke 6:37

Every time I walk into my office, I get a sense of pride. I look around at the company that I helped to build from the ground up and realize that it was obtainable because the Lord has *always* shown me Devine Favor. I learned the hard way to appreciate what I have and stop sweating the shit that I don't. Once I took this attitude, everything changed for me.

I work with one of my closest friends, Garrett Connors. He and I have worked together for some years and our thought process, to some degree, is about the same. He likes money and wants to make it as quick as possible. I like to be creative and bring things together so our very different viewpoints brings life to our business, Connors Gregory Partners. We started the business about three years ago, after we were both laid off. The best thing that ever could have happened to us was to lose those jobs. Correction - the jobs lost us! We used the unemployment benefits to get us through until we could start actually cashing some checks. The company specializes in strategic product marketing and placement and we have managed to generate revenue of over two-million dollars in the short time we have been in business. Not bad for a black-owned and operated business in Los Angeles.

Garrett is easy going, fun loving and keeps this office jumping. Today he's on the Lakers and how they better win the championship or he's sending Kobe and Phil packing. He personally feels that Luke should have *been* gone. But for the record; Kobe can't go nowhere. Matter of fact, it should be Kobe Bryant and the Los Angeles Lakers. You know, sort of like Smokey Robinson and the Miracles or Harold Melvin and the Blues Notes. Where the hell would the Lakers be without Kobe?

I'm a Lakers fan too but I like Bynum and Ariza. They're young, eager and full of the youthful energy that the Lakers have been in need of for some time. I use to feel sorry for them some years back when I would look at the bench and see nothing but dinosaurs. Who would ever dream that Shaq would leave the team and they would replace him with ~ hell who could replace Shaq? I had been thinking about sending the main office a letter but figured I would leave the coaching to the coaches; just make sure nobody's in my seat when I get to the game. I wish someone would be in my seat…

My assistant, Hunter Jefferson, pretty much runs the office when we are out conducting business, which is about eighty percent of the time. She's sharp, smart and keeps me on my toes. But Hunter can also be nosey, gossipy and overbearing if you allow her to be all in your business. With that said, she is one of the best people you will come across in Los Angeles.

"Karma, are you ready for your meeting at ten with Chambers and Associates? They have a huge project they're working on with some pretty influential people and they've requested for you to head the collaboration."

"I'm actually looking forward to it because we have been talking to them for months but have yet to have them bring us their business." I say while gathering my things.

"Hunter something real strange happened to me. I got this early morning call from someone name Erik who claims he worked with me on a product launch or something. Do you know Erik?"

"Yeah, I remember Erik and I'm surprised that you don't."

"Well why would I remember him and most importantly does he look half as good as he sounds on the phone?"

"Girrrl, he's a beautiful man! You didn't work directly with him so that's probably why you can't remember him. I'll say this, all while he was here I was making sure his coffe cup stayed full; I wanted him to know that I was born to make him happy." She jokes.

"You know you're too crazy Hunter, but I just can't remember anything about him."

"So how did he get your new phone number?" She smirks.

"You know, up until right now I thought he got it from you. Either way, we're going to dinner because I need the stimulation of having a conversation with a real grown man instead of Justin and Kyle. And being good looking is an added plus."

"Well then you go on Miss Thing! But don't do anything I wouldn't do. Don't want you walking around here all sprung."

***

Our meeting with Chambers and Associates went very well and the account is in the bag. Unfortunately, a one hour meeting turned into a three hour seminar and I can't get myself out the office in time to pick up the kids from school, go home and cook dinner, do some homework and go out with a man. Maybe it's not even time to start the whole dating thing anyway. Dating requires too much time and too much work ~ I'm not sure if I'm ready to work that hard. I really don't consider going out to dinner dating though, I consider it a free meal. A meal that I didn't have to cook; a meal I didn't have to pay for. I don't even remember the rules of dating anymore and I hear they've really changed. That was the good part about being married; I didn't have to go out on that awkward first date. Either way, I need to take a rain check because Thursdays are never good and I really could use a hot bath and a cup of tea (or a shot of Hennessey).

"You've reached the voicemail of Erik Gibson and I'm not available right now..." This man has such an amazing voice. He probably uses that voice to get every woman he runs into. Bet you I won't be a notch on this man's belt and why take me to dinner and you're not available – what the hell does that mean? The translation could possibly be *'I'm on the phone with another woman telling her some sweet shit about needing to take her to dinner and being honored to do it.'* Well he won't get the chance to play that game with me because I'm too old and too...

"Hi Erik, its Karma. I know we agreed to do dinner tonight but I need to cancel. It's been an awfully long day and I'm afraid I wouldn't be good company. Thank you for the offer but it's really just not a good night for me. Let's plan to get to get together real soon. You take care and let's be in touch."

***

I have to go see my father tonight before going home. Like I said this cancer thing is too much to handle. I try to stop by and spend time with him because I want him to know how much I love him and need him in my life. You know, my Daddy is the only man I have ever really loved. My Daddy is the only man I have ever really trusted. And my Daddy is the only man that has never disappointed me. He sets the standard for how I measure a man ~ a real man, that is. I love him so very much and it breaks my heart that I can't do anything to make the pain go away. Needless to say, my Daddy is my first love. And I'm truly a "*Daddy's Girl*".

"Hi Daddy, how are you feeling today?"

"You know baby girl, I'm not going to complain."

"Did you already eat today? And where is Momma?"

"She's in there somewhere and we had dinner already. Were my grandsons?"

Just when he asks the question, here comes Kyle and Justin. They simply adore their grandfather and he adores them too. Even in his state of health, he manages to mustard up enough strength to put them both in his lap. The boys know that there's something different about their Grandpa but what good would it do to tell them that he has cancer and may not be around forever; like I had planned (I had certainly planned that he would be here a good long time or even that I would go before he would). They wiggle and giggle in his lap for what seems like hours and finally my mother calls them into the kitchen to feed them some leftover dinner. Hallelujah! I don't have to cook after all. Thank God for Grandmas across the world!

"Baby Girl how are you *really* doing?"

He could always look into my eyes and know
that there was something wrong; read my entire soul in
just one glance. I have been carrying a big weight since
I asked Mister's low down, cheating ass to leave and it
must be apparent in my spirit. I could never fool my
Daddy though and he must know that I'm going through
the motions. The uncertainty is enough to drive me
insane at this point. I need to get this divorce final and
get on with my life. That's exactly what I will do – get
on with my life.

"Baby I don't know what happened between the
two of you but I got some advice for you, don't
straddle the fence. If you don't want him, let
him go. Don't argue, fight or judge him. You
can't fix him with all that foolishness; the way
you hurt a man is *simply* leave him alone. There
are plenty men out there looking for a woman
like you but you can't take the stuff you got from

this man to the next man. If you do that, you will always have a disaster on your hands. And always remember, when I'm dead and gone, that *you can't win with a loser.*"

I know God does things with His purpose and plan and I know He sent me here to see my father today for a reason. I needed to hear what my father had to say. Now I have to heed his advice to make a better life for myself and my children. As for Mister, I fault him for nothing and forgive him for everything. He just can't be married to me…

Right now it's like my heart is splitting in two because of my father's battle with cancer and the fear of what's to come (you didn't think I would be in the fetal position because of Mister, I know). I have never experienced a pain so deep that it takes my breath away. If, in fact, my father is dying, believe me so am I. I'm begging the Lord above to heal my Daddy. Lord knows it's too soon to call him home. *I'm praying…*

Chapter Four: Is She Serious?

*"Go, eat your bread with enjoyment, and drink your
wine with a merry heart; for God has already approved
what you do."*
Ecclesiates 9:7

    I have never been one for a bunch of foolishness;
has just never been my style. But this time Mister has
taken things way too far. I have gone out of my way to
make this whole co-parenting thing work to both our
advantage but he is always going against the grain. I
think he is personally trying to cause unnecessary
bullshit and chaos. If it's not one thing; it's another. I
think it's real cool for him to have a *girlfriend* but why
have her on my phone? With all the women and dumb
shit that Mister has done over the years, I could care less
about who he deals with because I know it will always
turn out the same way ~ fucked up!

    My theory is this; this woman was a secret all
while we were under the same roof so keep her ass a
secret now. But instead she's on the phone calling me
wanting to schedule a time for us to meet because

"eighteen years is a long time." She couldn't possibly think that Mister can keep his mask on for that long. She has left countless messages like she and I have something in common other than his fool ass. She really thinks she's hurting me by shacking up with my husband. *Is she serious?*

Mister didn't just get to be a low down asshole; he has always been a low down asshole but when he meets this girl, he changed instantly into the perfect man and husband. She has got to know that he can't be all that when he's married to me and living with her. He has a track record of meeting women and trying to destroy any glimmer of joy that they have. Put it to you like this: It was down right selfish for Mister to marry happy me knowing all the time that his ass was miserable and not fit for a woman – let alone a happy one.

Overall, I wish him the best and I guess that means that I have to return this girl's call and do this shit like we're not talking about my husband, *legally*. One thing I can say, Justin and Kyle hit it on the head when they said she was a ghetto hoochie. You should hear the message on her cell phone. She just can't be serious...

"Yeah you got Coretha, I know you want me so leave a message and let me know how you want it and I'll hit you back when I can get with you..."

I'm too old for this foolishness. Let's face it, I'm closer to fifty than I am fifteen and this shit reminds me of hanging under the bleachers in high school (minus the weed). What kind of message is that and what the hell is a Coretha? More importantly, she sounds like she's selling something and it's not Avon. All I can say is Mister really picked a real winner this time around. I leave a message and call it a day. She can call me back if she wants to and if not, it still won't be a problem for me. I'm finally going to meet Erik Gibson for dinner and I need to get myself together.

***

I'm looking at my watch. I know he said seven o'clock and its twenty minutes after and there's no sign of Erik. How would I know? Maybe he saw me and I wasn't his type so instead of suffering through dinner, he figured he would leave and just say forget it. But I'm looking good tonight so that couldn't possibly be it. My designer of choice is Via Spiga and tonight everything is working in perfect harmony. My hair ~ do I even need to say ~ is flawless. I'm doing my thing tonight and no sign of this mystery man. He has another ten minutes and I'm going to order my dinner and eat. That's that. I knew this was a bad idea when I agreed to it. See, I'm busy doing me and now here I sit waiting for some man I don't even know to pay for this meal. Don't get it twisted, I'm a go-getter so you know I'm paid, but I'm not in the mood to do dinner by myself. He has about another five minutes...

Oh my God! The most beautiful man in the world is walking my way. He is a straight chocolate brother, standing about six-three, his body is perfect

(I'm going to the gym tomorrow), he's neatly shaven and damn he looks so good. If he's not Erik, he should be. *Lord please let him be Erik...* Seems like it is taking forever for this man to walk through this room and his strut is making me sweat. Now I need to get a hold on myself because I'm doing way too much. This is about having dinner with a nice man and having good conversation. It's not about imaging the many positions that I can sex this man in. It's not about the last couple of months with no sex. No, it's not about all that but it damn sure could be by the end of the night.

"Karma, girl you look good." he said with his arms extended for a hug.

I would be wrong not to hug this man but I can hardly stand up because my knees are weak from him walking over here. I have to get up or look like a complete fool but shit he better wait. He knew when he was walking through here making every woman's head turn that it was going to be hard for me to stand. And then I don't know if I want this hug. I'm scared. But I rise and give him a hug. I think you should know that he smells like I imagined. Everything on this man is rock solid and I love this but I guess the embrace is over now. Damn I got to let him go. Probably would be a good idea to even speak ~ say something. Anything...

"So Erik, finally I get to put a face with the voice," there I said something.

"Karma, I have been thinking about you all while I was out of town. You left me with such an impression that I was eager to get back and just be in your presence so I'm going to just sit here and look at you all evening, if you don't mind." He says with a smile.

Now that's some real smooth shit there and the feeling is mutual. All of a sudden I get this urge to be the very best I can be; he deserves something truly special. And why is this waiter hanging around this table anyway; doesn't he have an order to take? I guess he wants us to order dinner, huh? Well the BBQ spare ribs are out. I always get my favorite spare ribs when I come here but its time to pick a new favorite. Something I can eat that makes me look sexy. Yeah, I said it ~ "sexy". I'll have the half shell oysters but that may be a little too direct and I certainly don't want him to get the impression that I'm some kind of whore whose going to take him down on an instant ~ on the first night with nothing but dinner and conversation; damn he looks good.

"I'll have the grilled salmon and baked potato," I say to the waiter.

"Have you ever tried the spare ribs? They are my favorite." He said while gesturing to the waiter

"No. I don't eat pork."

I can't figure out what made me say that. I eat pork all the time and he's going to be sitting across the table from me eating my favorite spare ribs because I was too chicken to take a risk and lick my fingers in front of him. Licking your fingers can be very sexy too, right? What the hell was I thinking!

Okay now for the small talk until our meals come. I'm going to keep looking at this wine list until he says something. It is so awkward to be meeting someone for the first time and not knowing exactly what to say. I certainly don't want to show my hand too soon so I'll wait for him to start the conversation.

When his lips move, I don't hear a word he says. This man is so incredibly sexy. His lips are perfect! His teeth are perfect! His eyes are a soft brown and only compliment his bushy eyebrows. I think I'm supposed to speak but I have been so caught up with watching his mouth move that I am oblivious to everything he has said. I would look like an idiot asking him to repeat everything so I'm going to wing it. The uncomfortable smile and a small laugh is my response… Yeah, I look like a complete idiot.

"So you did or didn't run into traffic getting here?" He asked again.

"Oh no, I didn't hit any traffic. I can imagine you did though."

"Nope. I'm just late." He replies.

He's just late. No excuses, just late. *Late*. I fed two kids and tucked them in; briefed a baby sitter; sent out an email blast to my staff; washed a load of clothes; wrote my grocery list, paid my bills online, ironed the boys' clothes for tomorrow, called Danica to let her know where I would be tonight and stopped to fill up my tank and still made it here on time. Is this a sign that this man is not for me? Who said he was "for me" anyway. Why am I even tripping? I'm here for the meal and conversation only. That's it and his being late and not giving a shit makes the deal even sweeter. But he is sexy...

"You make it a habit to be late and waste people's valuable time? Or do you think that you're such a gift to women that we will all wait for the great Erik to arrive?" I ask.

"Karma, it's not like that at all. I remember during our initial meeting that you said you collect elephants so I stopped by this wood shop to get this." talking while he's reaching into his pocket.

He pulls out the cutest wooden elephant with the most exquisite hand-carved details. This elephant is simply beautiful. And he remembered that much about me from our meeting; our initial meeting that I don't even remember. If I didn't feel like an idiot earlier, I certainly do now. This man has paid attention and taken the time to figure out what I would like; he remembered one of the smallest details. This man must be feeling me something terrible and here I am getting ready to truly set if off. Have I gotten so use to Mister and his lame ass that I think every man is out to get me?

"Erik this is really something. Thank you so much. I'm speechless."

"You're more than welcome and I wanted you to be speechless. It helps when I'm trying to impress you."

At this point he could have me anyway he wants me. Really he could. Just reel me in because I'm hooked. Boy I'm glad I decided to wait for him. After meeting him, I would wait here in this very spot, at this very table, all damn night. Go ahead, be late ~ you're worth the wait! That's real. I thought the dinner would be the high point of the evening, but instead it's Erik. I'm sitting here looking into his eyes wondering would I ever get married again because if I did, I would want my husband to be just like him. I would want him to be someone who pays attention to my needs, knows what I like, can wear a pair jeans like he does and wouldn't hurt if he was drop dead fine, just like Erik. I'm so superficial…

We talk for what seems like hours only to have to end the date (*yes, it is a date*). Reality is I could spend the rest of the night talking with him and laughing about some of the things that make you raise an eyebrow. I have to be to work early tomorrow morning for a conference call and should have been home hours ago, but I have been unable to pull myself away from this table, this conversation, this man. For the first time in my life, I'm concerned about if a man will call me tomorrow. I know I'm tripping.

"Thank you so much for dinner. I really enjoyed the conversation and the walk down memory lane. We will have to do it again some time." I say with confidence.

"We will have to do it again and again and again." He replies. "Can I call you tomorrow?"

There he goes again with that smooth shit again. *Can he call me?* Boy please, he needs to stop. He'd better be on my phone or I will be on his. I'll be at his front door. I'll be sending emails with smiley faces. I'll be peeking from behind bushes at his office and the whole nine. Stalking his fine ass like it's the thing to do. Sure he can call. Call me... *please.* What if he doesn't? He will. He better... Will he call me when he gets a chance?

"Well I will have a few minutes free tomorrow afternoon so if you get a minute, do call me." I say.

I couldn't very well say, "Please call me." That just wouldn't go over well. And I couldn't beg him to call, so there wasn't anything left to say. As we walk outside into the night air, something very calming comes over me. I realize that I'll be okay. I realize that I'm not wrong to want the attention of a man and have a natural attraction to him.

I also realize that if he doesn't let go of my hand, I'm going to give him some! How do I even know he wants some? Well if he wants some, it's his. Matter of fact he gets the triple deluxe – maybe not that because I couldn't do all that the first time out. That would only be nasty. Way too nasty matter of fact. We have plenty of time for that because I will make myself a priority in his life. This is going to be good. Watch and see. I'm thankful that God made this man call me in the middle of the night and I didn't go off on him. *And now I believe in love at first sight...*

Chapter Five: Is That The Phone?

"Let us hold fast the confession of our hope without wavering, for He who promised is faithful"
Hebrews 10:23

It's a bad wind that never realizes it's time for a change. I have allowed my frustration and the uncertainty to turn me into a cursing maniac. I have to get a grip and control what I say, even though Mister and his whore have made it hard to do anything else but curse. I finally spoke to Coreatha and I must admit, she wasn't as bad as I anticipated. Matter fact she was amiable and seemed to be genuinely concerned about the boys' well-being, especially when they're in her care. I realize that my problem is not with this her but instead with Mister. I don't have any type of beef with Coretha ~ I married Mister and he betrayed me; my problem is with his bitch-made ass!

In talking to Coreatha, she told me how Mister wished me nothing but bad luck. How crazy is that? I guess it has never dawned on him that I'm the mother of his two children and if I suffer, so do they. Still this is how he wants to play it so Coreatha and I agree that she will pick up the boys every Wednesday after school and Mister will return them after they have dinner. Not a problem; all this means is that the chef has the night off. If she can extend herself for my children, I can certainly meet her half way. I'll have to see what happens.

Meanwhile, Erik and I have been playing telephone tag for the past few days. I can't understand why we can't seem to connect but I'm eager to talk to him. Our date went well and to be honest, I want to get all these awkward dates out of the way so that I can see what the man is really about. From an intellectual stand point I know he's at the top of his game, but I need to know what he's *really* like. Then there is that side of me that thinks maybe he's just not that in to me after all and rather than hurt my feelings, he would rather avoid me and unknowingly piss me off. Either way, I will give him one more call and then I'm done. I refuse to wait until I'm full grown to go running and chasing behind some man; I have two children to chase after if chasing is what I want to do. Why would my fine ass pursue a man so tough just to get a simple "hello"? Once I leave this final message, the ball is certainly in his court. If he calls, he calls. If he doesn't, then fuck him (I really have to stop cursing).

I dial his number and it rings; rings again and then again. Okay let me leave a message that will spark his interest and make him think about what he's missing out on. Just as I'm prepared to leave my message, he answers.

"Hi Karma, I'm so glad you called."

"Seems like we have been missing each other every since our date. How have you been?" I ask.

"Busy and hating the fact that I don't have time to get to know you better."

"Well you know how to make an impression on a woman and then leave her hanging."

"That was never my intentions, so please give me a chance to see what makes a lady like you tick..."

Since we're on the topic of intentions, what exactly are his intentions? I mean we haven't seen each other since our date. We haven't spoken since that night. We've played telephone tag for what seems like forever (but it's really about eight days), and now he mentions something about intentions. I'm so use to men having there intentions so mapped out by day eight that we both know what they want and how bad they want it. But Erik is different ~ he's not tripping off of rushing into anything. He's just not in a hurry. Maybe he's procrastinating or maybe he's just believes in taking his time. I need to know what his intentions are so that I can prepare myself.

"So you have some intentions for me, Erik?"

"Yeah, I must say I do and as soon as things slow down for me, I plan on letting you in on them all." He laughs.

"Would I be too bold to say I would love to see you and that you have crossed my mind about a million times since we met."

"Being straight forward is a trait I admire and I feel the same way. I was actually wondering if I was being a little school boyish because I have been sitting here day dreaming about your smile and replaying in my mind the conversation we had over dinner. And there are so many things I want to know about you Karma, like what's your favorite color? Are you a Republican or Democrat? Regular or Decaf..." He says with a smile in his voice.

"My favorite color is red, I'm a Democrat and I prefer my coffee strong, black and sweet. Is there anything else?" I ask.

This man doesn't have a clue that I would give him all of me and I don't even know him. I'm not caring about what anyone would think about my next move. My heart wants to be loved in a new way and I know that in order to find the love that I need and deserve, I'm going to have to take some risk. I might even need to step my game up to some degree. For the most part, I'm not worried about nobody but myself; nobody is worried about me. Like I said, all the rules have changed. I got to change with them.

"So when will I see you again, Karma? I was thinking I could cook you dinner and we could have movie night at my house. You can even bring the boys with you if you want. And before you answer, I know you're busy with work but there has to be some time that you can set aside for me and I promise not to keep you too long. What do you say?"

"There's no way I'm bringing my kids with me especially if you value your belongings but I'm open to whatever, so let me know by the end of the week."

"I can let you know right now. Would Friday work for you? I'll pick you up" he says.

"Friday sounds good but you have to let me bring something; a bottle of wine or something."

"All you have to bring is you. I think I can handle everything else..."

He's blatantly flirting with me. Some smooth shit too, if I must say myself ~ all I have to bring is myself. I'm with that though. As usual, I'm too fucking slow to come back with something silky and sexy. All I can say is "okay" like a damn fool. He has to think I'm so retarded. I still regret not ordering the ribs when we went out to dinner and now I can't even flirt back. What the hell is wrong with me? Maybe I'm putting too much on it but I want it to be more that just another date; more than just another woman he has met. I want to be a true priority in his life. I could easily be his woman, his boo, *his period*...

Don't get me wrong; I know that he was doing something and someone as recent as a couple of weeks ago. You know a man always has some ass he can call ~ kind of like pussy on demand. And we women can dial-a-dick at any given time too so we don't help matters. I want to be so much more than that though. This man has me wide open. Can he really handle everything else? I come with a lot of shit right now and it may even be selfish for me to attempt to establish something with him when I know what I'm going through with dumb ass Mister. I have needs and wants and right now, I need and want some Erik more than anything in the world. Real or not, I need to be in this man's arms. I can't be wrong for needing that. We're both consenting adults and fuck it; I need to get mine while the getting is good.

We agree to Friday evening at seven o'clock. He will pick me up from my house ~ now I'm really tripping. I didn't know men still pick women up from the house; plus I don't like everybody knowing where I live. I'll have to make sure that Justin and Kyle have all their toys up from all over the house. I guess I should probably clean the mutha fucka up – it wouldn't hurt to run the vacuum and mop the floor. Exactly! I will actually give the house a quick go over so he doesn't think I'm some nasty bitch, you know. He even had the nerve to tell me to think about him until we're together again. I'm such a sucka for a smooth line. Got me on one! My dreams will be sweet tonight; too bad I'm sleeping alone.

***

"Karma, your husband's on line three. Do you want to take the call or should I send him to voicemail?"

"I'll take the call because he's supposed to pick up the boys from school and I don't need the foolishness tonight so I'll take it – This is Karma Bernard".

"So you're using your maiden name now huh?"

"What can I do for you Adam? Are you still getting the boys from school?"

"Oh yeah everything is cool. Coreatha will get them as soon as they get out. I thought I would just call and see how you've been?"

"I've been happy. Thank you for your concern. I've got to go."

Fuck Mister and the horse he road in on! He has never cared how I was doing. Had he cared he would have changed some shit when he had a chance. I'm not trying to talk about anything with him but my children.

That's the only topic we can come to some form of agreement on so let's stick with what works. Avoid the headache. I haven't given him any energy, arguing, bitching, complaining or face time since we separated. His simple ass is Coreatha's problem now and I don't owe him anything but a good dose of "left alone". I will not allow him in my head today anyway because a real man is on my mind on this day that the Lord has made. He better make sure he picks my children up on time because if he doesn't, he and his hood rat bitch will be more than sorry. *They don't want to start no shit with me...*

Chapter Six: Could This Be?

"But as for me, I walk in my integrity; redeem me, and
be gracious to me."
Psalms 26:11

I feel sixteen again. It seems like I have been getting ready for my evening with Erik all week. I went to the salon and got the hair all whipped up; there's not a strand out of place. My next stop is the nail salon to get something done to these hands and feet. Got myself a fresh eyebrow arching because it makes no sense to have everything working and have a complete Unna brow to scare the man, you hear what I'm saying?

Figured since I was there, I might as well get my underarms and legs waxed. Matter of fact, I got the hook up! Don't need hair downtown either; wouldn't want a brotha to get hair in his teeth. Let's be real for a minute, it's kind of nasty to have all that hair and then expect a man to want to dine at Matilda's. With all that goes on in a run of a month with us, a man already has a lot of nerves to even contemplate such an act anyway. If the tables were turned and I was a man, a woman would certainly be on her own with all of that. If she couldn't lick it herself, she would be shit out of luck. Believe that.

I do, however, have very high expectation for tonight's dinner. I'm impressed that Erik can cook. I'm getting a little ahead of myself. His food could taste like old shoes, who knows? I'm still impressed that he would try to impress me by cooking. I'm digging him so tough that he could actually boil some old shoes and fry some straw hat, and because it's him, I would politely ask him to pass the hot sauce. Damn right!

But tonight I will simply follow his lead and if it leads to something; I'm ready. If it leads to nothing at all, I can deal will that too. My ninety day rule has just been pumped up to about nineteen days. I don't give a damn what Steve Harvey has to say! I'm suppose to think like a man and act like a lady when just the thought of this man, not to mention the sound of his voice, has my panties wet. That's easy for Steve to say. Tonight I'm going to act like I'm horny and think like a man ~ get me some if this man offers it up.

And I'm looking good. Plainly dressed in a Aomeiko Design T-shirt and jeans – that should do it. Can't forget the stilettos. An outfit is just not complete without them. Me and all my girls work the hell of these damn things, especially when we don't have to stand up all night. I'm ready. Now all he has to do is ring the door bell. I guess I'll just sit here and watch the First 48 episodes that I recorded last week. This man is late. *Again...*

***

I can hear someone on my porch, kind of scuffling around. It must be Erik. He's late as it is and now he's not going to ring the door bell. Why do men always do stupid shit? He needs to stop playing! This man just may be some serial killer – you know Black men are doing that shit now. He could be a serial rapist (that's taking it a bit far, he doesn't have to rape nobody with the way he has it going on). He could simply be a stupid mutha fucka that doesn't know how to tell time and could give a hot fuck about the next person's schedule. He better ring this damn door bell already.

"Is someone out there?" I ask.

"Yeah Karma, it's me – Erik"

"And there's a reason why you're on the other side of the door, right?"

"Well, because you haven't opened it."

"Because you haven't rung the door bell."
(Ding, dong, ding, dong)

"Now I have," He says with a giggle.

I open the door and there he is. As usual he is so worth the wait. Damn, he is the sexiest man that I have ever seen. He makes a white Tee and Levi's look like

Sunday's best. He's smiling that perfect smile and holding a single red rose. He starts to recite poetry…

> *"She is only a rose, nothing more or less. Her scent is to captivate the many that will cross her path but her thorns are to protect her heart. Her petals are only a small part of her beauty. For it is her inside; this is where her true beauty radiates. She is only a rose, nothing more or less."*

I wonder if this was written just for me or does he have plenty of the good shit in his bag of tricks. I can't help but wonder. I want so bad to trust him and think that everything he does is especially for me. I want to believe that we're a special pair and that he is feeling me the way I'm feeling him. There is something so sincere in his eyes. His smile is genuine. And his hug only makes me feel certain that I deserve the love this man has to offer. *Could this be?*

"I wrote that just for you Karma," he says hugging me tight.

All I feel is muscles. This is truly like embracing a brick wall. Every inch of this man is in top shape. At some point I'm going to have to let him go but I sure want to stay right here in his arms. His hug can actually be my dinner. I don't need anything to eat anyway and after feeling his rock solid body, I'm in the gym first thing tomorrow morning. Really. I refuse to go out like this so I'm going to get my ass in the gym and shed the twenty pounds that I have been losing for the past nine months. Yes, I have made up my mind, Erik and I will look like Black Barbie and Ken...

"I'm impressed. Do you write poetry all the time?"

"I use to in college but now, I rarely run into people who appreciate poetry."

"Well I do so please test your material on me."

"I'll take you up on that. You have a beautiful home Karma. Did you do all the decorating yourself?"

Now he's being ridiculous. Mister would have never allowed me to get a decorator; I almost didn't get furniture. My home is something I'm very proud of because of the mere fact that I was able to hand-select every single item under the roof. Plus, I have been polishing and shining all week because I wanted to make a good impression. It worked. So I guess next he'll want a tour, we'll end up in my bedroom and next thing I know I'll miss out on dinner.

"I would love to see the whole house but maybe next time because I have to get you to my place so I can charm you with my gourmet meal."

"I'm ready. Let me just grab my coat and set my alarm."

Well he's not predictable that's for sure. My heart is dancing now. I like being wrong about Erik. It means he is at least coming up with some brand new shit instead of the same old smoke up my ass, you know. Being a typical woman, I want something to be wrong with him. I can't just let him be a nice man who wants to get to know me better. He can't just be a man who's not playing games and all that dumb stuff. I really need to stop and just enjoy the company and attention of this fine man instead of over analyzing everything and trying to anticipate his next move.

"Where did you park your car?"

"I'm parked across the street. I wasn't sure if you were one of those people who gets all bent out of shape when people park in your driveway."

It would have been good for him to park as close to the door as possible; I haven't been in these stilettos for what seems like forever so I have to get my walk together. It's like a balancing act but I'm going to make the shit sexy. All the way across the street, huh? Well, I'm looking good; smelling good ~ shit tonight, I'm just plain good!

I know Erik is not driving this beat up Ford Taurus. He couldn't be driving that car not looking like he looks. He just can't be. That doesn't even matter. He's a sweet man and he's interesting, so I don't care what he rolled up here in because it's the man that makes the car and not the other way around. I just pictured him in a Benz or a Lexus, something down those lines. I would have never in my wildest dream thought that he would be driving an older model Ford Taurus. I'm tripping…

"Down this way Karma, maybe I should have taken a chance and pulled in the driveway but I see you're a professional" he says while pointing down to my shoes.

"Yeah I have gotten pretty good over the years."

"I think stilettos are the sexiest thing a woman can wear. Here's my car right here, let me get the door for you."

That's what I'm talking about! I should have known that Erik wouldn't be caught dead in that Ford. But this car, well it looks like it was made for him. One of my favorite cars too, I must add. Not everyday you see a convertible Boxster and this one doesn't even have a license plate. It's brand new. I hope he's not looking for help with the payment on this damn thing because I'm not the one. What about my hair? I can't ride with this top down, plus I'm scared. Someone may get in here on us and then we're ass out.

"Here baby, put this on so you won't mess up your hair." He says while passing me a baseball cap, "Unless you want me to put up the top."

"I'm cool. It's a great evening to ride with the top down. Don't worry about me."

***

Fabulous! That's the only word to describe this house. The walls are mint green and there is a scent of jasmine in the air. It's really odd that a man's house would smell like jasmine. Apparently, he is a man that takes excellent care of himself and likes the finer things in life. I hope that this is not a sign of selfishness or worse – homosexuality! Either that or there is a woman hiding in one of these damn rooms. This house just couldn't be that of a single man ~ it's too perfect.

"Karma, please feel free to look around. I need to get your dinner started so please make yourself at home baby."

What's up with all this "baby" stuff? And stop playing, if you want me to make myself at home, give me a key. I know how to make myself at home alright. I will be hanging pictures of me and my kids over your fireplace, picking out patio furniture and answering your phone so don't tell me to make myself at home.

"I'll do that. I would love to see if you can get any better than when I first entered the door."

"Baby, I've poured your wine so take off your shoes and come get your glass too."

"From the aroma, you must know what you're doing. I just love a man that can cook."

"And I just love a woman that appreciates that I can cook."

"What are you cooking anyway – its making me so hungry?"

"It's a surprise so go give your self the grand tour, baby. I'll meet you in the den in a minute."

There he goes with that "baby" thing again. I wonder if he calls every woman baby. I'm upstairs looking around and stumble on to a complete princess room. This room is what every little girl dreams about. The canopy bed and white teddy bear ballerinas with a pink chandelier that sparkles as the light hits the crystals. A room fit for a little princess. I can really appreciate this room but who the hell sleeps here? *Erik couldn't sleep here.* He hasn't mentioned any kids as many times as I have mentioned my boys. See this is where the bullshit comes in. I need to see the other rooms. Relax.

This room with the plasma television and all the remotes must be Erik's room. There's a Newsweek and a Sports Illustrated on the night stand. He can read ~ Yippy! There are also a couple of business cards and a woman's tennis bracelet on the dresser, along with several bottles of Creed for men. In case you don't know, Creed runs about two hundred dollars a bottle. Apparently, Erik likes the fragrance a lot and if he's wearing it tonight, I like it too. Got to stay up on these things.

"I see you found my bedroom."

"Yeah, I did and your home is amazing. Looks like a woman took special care in decorating and all, especially the little girl's room…"

"Yeah, I'm raising my niece; my brother's daughter. My brother was killed in a drive-by shooting when his girlfriend was pregnant. She sort of went off the deep end after that and I adopted Bailey because it was pretty obvious that her mother wasn't going to be able to raise her. She loves her room too."

"That's real big of you to take on the responsibility of raising her alone. I know it gets hard."

"Well dinner is ready, unless you want to hang out here while I eat. Can I get another hug?"

Holding this man in my arms seems so right. He's an honorable man with strong principles. Why didn't I meet him ten years ago when I was in baby making mode? I know he is a great father to his niece. I hope Erik feels the same way I do. *I'm hooked...*

***

I know why he was late; he had to make preparations for this great meal. We had strawberry, almond and spinach salad, heavenly snapper and for desert he made a pecan love tart. That's what he called it. The dinner was delicious. I could have had seconds but I don't want him to think I'm a greedy bitch gobbling up all his food. I'm so awed by him... But if we're going to watch movies, I hope he has one that's not bootleg. I hate bootlegs, they're always hard to see and someone's head is always in the way.

"Did you see Notorious while it was in the theaters?" he asked while filing through a stack of damn bootlegs.

"No I didn't. Someone gave me a bootleg copy and it was terrible so I never watched it..."

"Well that kills that because I have the bootleg copy too. Tell you what, let's watch Training Day or Dream Girls – pick one..." He says holding up both movies.

"Training Day, hands down."

"Now what do you have against Beyonce?"

"I don't have anything against her but I have to take her and that movie in doses. I have to be in the mood for all of that."

We cuddle watching Denzel and it seems so right. The movie is funny as hell to me because I have a warped sense of humor (I guess hell isn't really that funny, especially if you live there). Picture this; it's your first day on a new job. You meet your new boss who appears to be pretty cool on the surface and she says she's going to train you on everything you'll need to know about your role and responsibilities. You start your training by first getting high off of ecstasy, then robbing a local resident of Nickerson Gardens, kill a seemingly innocent man and take his money, and then you're left with a group of Mexican assassins to fin for yourself. Fuck being in ~ do you think I really want to work here now? Talk about a long day at the office. Anyway...

We talk through the first half of the movie and I fall asleep by the second half. I hope I wasn't snoring...

Damn, I was snoring! I can tell by the way he's looking at me. I get so tired sometimes that when I finally go to sleep – it's ugly. I get that ugly feeling right now. How uncomfortable. Ever wanted to get away?

"Baby, the movie is over. You missed half of it."

"Was I snoring?"

"That's what that was? I didn't know what you were doing; I just didn't want to get in your way. Seems like it would have gotten violent." He say while laughing.

"I'm so embarrassed. I apologize for falling asleep and snoring and…"

"No need to apologize. It's all good. Don't worry about all that. Let's just go to bed."

Go to bed? That wasn't part of the deal. I know I said I wanted to get me some but I was just playing. I hope he doesn't think that I'm willing to pay for my meal in pussy. I didn't say anything about working for food. You never know what a man is thinking. He is sexy though and I'm full grown. I can do what my heart feels and if I can live with myself in the morning, everyone else should be able to. Plain and simple, I can fuck this man tonight if I'm good and damn ready. And I'm good and damn ready! *I think...*

"Karma, you look worried but I want to assure you that I'm not in a rush to make love to you, even though I'm digging you. I want you to see the beauty of being friends first and that requires some time, so I'm not going to press you to do anything. You can even sleep in Bailey's room if you want but please don't make me take you all the way home tonight..."

"I'm not worried and I would love to be your house guest but I have to get home early in the morning, so you promise…"

"Yes, I will take you home as soon as your eyes open in the morning." He grabs my hand and leads me upstairs.

Could this be? I think I should be insulted that he's not trying to get some. He's really not. Matter of fact, I think he's already sleep. Damn, that was quick. He goes to sleep on his way down to the pillow. It must be around two in the morning, so being tired is expected. He's even fine when he sleeps. I haven't forgotten about the tennis bracelet on the dresser or how he conveniently didn't even acknowledge the comment about his decorator. Why trip? His T-shirt is a perfect fit, in terms of sleeping in my man's T-shirt. *Yeah, my man.* There's only one problem with this perfect evening; only one true red flag. His phone has never stopped vibrating. I think I know what that's all about.

Whoever "*she is*", she wants him to answer the phone and thinks that continuously calling him is going to make him answer. I'm not tripping because she's on his phone but I'm the queen of this throne tonight. She might as well go her ass to sleep, *I know I am...*

Chapter Seven: Is Everything Okay?

Consider the work of God: who can make straight what
He has made crooked"
Ecclesiastes 7:13

Erik drops me off at home like he promised. The kiss at my front door makes me want to kick my own ass ~ I know I should have given him some last night! But now he knows I'm a lady and he will continue to treat me like one. I think giving him a couple of humps of this good stuff would have had the man sucking his thumb anyway. One never knows, he may not even be able to hang. I'm the first to say that women these days are sexually liberated and I'm leading the army. Anyway, there's absolutely nothing wrong with a woman being sexually confident and knowing she can put it down, right?

The evening with him was simply incredible. For him to respect me and not pressure me into anything makes it even better. Even had the nerve to call me once he got back into the car. We must have talked for another hour or so as he drove home. I'm really digging this man, *my man*...

Now it's back to reality. I check my messages and Coreatha has called me at least six or seven times this morning. I wonder what that's all about. I know there better not be anything wrong with my kids or this bitch will get the ass kicking that I have been saving just for her. She and Mister know better than to mess with me about my boys. I better call her back.

"Hello Coreatha, its Karma. Is everything okay? Are the boys alright?"

"Karma, the boys are fine. It's Adam, he's in the hospital. Seems like there's something wrong with his lungs – they think its pneumonia. He was having problems breathing this morning and was taken by ambulance to the hospital for observation. They need to run some test and see what can be done to regulate his breathing. And he was having some sort of chest pains. I'm so scared…"

"Now Coreatha, Adam will be fine girl. Don't even sweat that."

"Can you do me a big favor?"

"What's that?"

"Do you think you can pick up the boys early so that I can get to the hospital and speak with the doctor? I don't think they want to see their father in the hospital" she says.

"Certainly, I'm on my way. Tell them to get they're things together and meet me outside."

"Thanks Karma."

"No problem, see you in about twenty minutes. And if there is anything you need me to do, please let me know girl."

I have to exchange pleasantries but I really have no intentions of getting involved with Mister and any of his chaos. He's probably faking, like he always does, to get out of doing something that he promised. He has always conveniently gotten sick when it comes time to honor his word or commitment. Mister is Coreatha's problem now but I will pick up my children so that he can milk this situation for what it's worth.

There is some good that comes out of his Oscar-winning performance. She has managed to do in a couple of months, what I couldn't do over five years ~ get Mister to see a doctor. He's in the hospital and that's never good but I'm sure it's nothing but a little heart burn. All devils are able to handle a little heat so I'm sure his ass will be just fine.

***

All I can do is day dream about Erik all the way home. The boys are arguing about something but I can't even focus long enough to referee today. The evening with Erik was incredible. I may sound a little school-girlish but I'm just going to wait until he calls me. I sense that he's not the type of man who get's hung up on who calls who but I'm still a little bit old school in terms of calling in behind a man. My cell phone is ringing and I know its Danica. She had left a message on my machine asking where the hell I was early in the morning. She just did that to see if I had spent the night with Erik. I know because she never ever calls me before noon. She's being nosey.

Danica Lawrence is one of my closet friends and she is because she understands me and never holds anything against me. As a girlfriend, she allows me to be myself and never ask me to change or compromise how I feel about things. She's married for the third time to a man, who on the surface, appears to be perfect. Although Danica doesn't seem that happy, I keep praying for them because families are meant to be together. She has two kids too – both girls though. So you can imagine how goofy Kyle and Justin get when they come to visit for the day. She and I met while working in the same hell hole as Garrett and I. One thing I must say about the hell hole, it attracted some really good people.

I know that Danica is snooping because she has been asking me how I live a life of celibacy after having an active sex life. To her, to go without sex for seven days would be a true struggle. She can call it celibacy but I call it "better safe than sorry". The real issue about celibacy is respecting a person's choice. My choice, up until this point, is based on the factual understanding of my options. Too many people base their choice to be celibate on some false guilt, rooted in religious teachings that were put in place to control people, *sexually*. I'm the first one to say, sex can get out of control and quickly. I think some people that decide to be celibate are also hiding deeper fears of intimacy. I know for me, sex can make me vulnerable in ways that I rather not be and make me start thinking with a different part of my brain.

Unknown to Danica, I stopped fucking Mister some time ago. After I found out that he would fuck anybody (and I do mean anybody!), I realized that I had to protect myself. It was life or death – I chose life! Hey, I only have one me and why take the risk of getting some shit from him when I already know he's cheating; and just could be gay for all I know. I don't see the sense in that so I stopped even thinking about sex. So Danica wants to know if I got some last night. That's all.

"Hey Danica, now what do I owe the pleasure of your call?"

"You know what I want heffa, what was it like?"

"What was what like?"

"Didn't you go to dude's house for dinner last night?"

"Yeah, oh he's an excellent cook. Girl the dinner and company was both delicious…"

"Now you know I'm not talking about that! How was the bedroom action, I know you took a brotha down so tell me something."

"Danica, there comes a time in everyone's life when they have to grow the fuck up. This time is your time!"

"So it was that damn good that you can't even talk about it?"

"Your ass is crazy. We didn't do all that. I went over there for dinner. We watched a movie, I fell asleep…"

"You fell asleep? Oh shit, why did you do that? You know how you snore."

"I didn't purposely fall asleep but shit I was tired and full. We were watching Training Day and next thing I know I was sleep. He said my snoring was cool."

"Yeah he said that but I'm telling you – you sound like a man sleeping off a buzz in the county jail. You know he's not going to mess with you after all that…" She laughs.

"Anyway, I had to pick the boys up from Mister early because this fool is faking some kind of illness so that his bitch will… You know what I will call you back because I have the boys in the car with me now."

"Don't nobody want to hear nothing about Mister's homosexual ass anyway! Fuck him! I want to hear more about Erik. Did you guys at least do some humping? And why in the hell were you two watching Training Day. Denzel won an Oscar for that in what year? Brotha needs to update his DVD collection quickly. He didn't have a movie that was released in say the last five years? Talk about digging in the crates. Come on now Karma…"

"Girl if you don't get off my phone. I'll get back to you later today or when I get to work on Monday. Talk to you later."

***

Before we can walk in the door good, I give the boys a pop quiz. I can't even say that I'm not curious to know what happened to Mister. Somewhere deep inside, I'm worried. I know I talk a lot of shit about Mister but reality is, he is the father of my children and I know they need him, even if I can't stand him.

"So your dad is sick, what happened?"

"He couldn't breath and his chest was hurting so Coreatha called 9-1-1."

"Yeah, he was turning all blue and stuff. It was scary Mommy" Justin spurts out.

"Is he going to be okay Mom?" Kyle questions.

"All we can do is wait and see what the doctors say but I'm sure its nothing. He will be fine, you just wait and see."

Mister is so needy; dramatic ass...

Chapter Eight: What Did You Just Say?

*"Vindicate me, O Lord, for I have walked in my
integrity, and I have trusted in the
Lord without wandering"*
Psalms 26:1

Have you ever looked at Florida and James Evans; I mean really took a good look at them? I have. What the hell would make anyone think that the two of them were ever having a good time in a pile of shit? This woman's life with this lazy bastard was riddled with chaos and confusion and *this was in the late seventies*. Not just on one or two episodes, but each and every one. Every time there seemed to be a light at the end of the tunnel, something would come through to fuck it all up. Like the time when they were moving from the projects back to Mississippi. Not that this would be a move forward but it would certainly be a move out of the projects – sort of like jumping out of the frying pan square into the fire.

Anyway, they planned to leave Chicago and the project residents decide to give them a farewell party.

During the celebration, a telegram was received from Mississippi letting Florida and the kids know that James was killed in a train accident. With that, the Evans' plans were foiled and they remained in the projects another two seasons or so.

On a later episode, Thelma meets and plans to marry Keith, who's headed to the NFL, and he will rescue her and the Evans family. They get married only for him to get hurt at the wedding and, as luck would have it, he never makes it to training camp. Instead he moves into the projects with the Evans family. Damn! Always some funky bullshit! Who has that kind of luck? Most importantly, who came up with the concept for the show ~ to be so heartless and develop a script of nothing but torture for a woman and call it Good Times?

Like most women; especially Black women, Florida's ass went through straight hell in the name of love. I say that because James was just a little too content in the projects raising his kids; always running around in those corduroys with an attitude talking shit. And I can not recall one episode when Florida's nerves weren't bad and when she was not stressed the fuck out. It shouldn't have to be like that...

Although that's only Hollywood at work, I know people who live the same type of lifestyle with a trifling, lazy ass man. By no means am I bashing men but I think I got lucky with Erik. He's a real man with integrity and pride; a prayer answered. Really he is. In the past I would rush to the wrong conclusions about men but this time, I'm willing to put money on it. The last couple of weeks have been like an intellectual fantasy. I say "intellectual" because there hasn't been much conversation about sex, not really. I have mentioned it a couple of times but he seems dead set on knowing who I am and forming a mental connection before jumping in the hay. That's some new shit for me. Don't get it twisted, I'm with all of that but I've already been sexless for going on fourteen months and counting; so I'm ready for something to jump off. Trust that.

Meanwhile, I know Erik is digging me. We see each other at least twice a week. That's a lot for two people with hectic schedules and shit to do. This man unselfishly brings bags of grocery to my house and cooks me dinner while I soak in the tub. He hangs out with his boys but nothing extreme and more importantly he's not smoking blunts and getting loaded when he does. I simply hate that shit!

Needless to say, we're both Lakers fans and as of the end of this season, we're also season ticket holders. Now that's what I'm talking about. Erik is exciting and fun loving. He even helped Justin and Kyle plant a garden in the back yard. Check this out, my boys love Erik and I think he loves them. They really need that right now.

I have to be honest with you; there is something to be said for loving someone mentally, *first*. You think I may be on to something? And how profound huh ~ become friends before screwing his brains out, wow…

Right now, my heart has no fear. With Erik, my heart is safe. I can relax. To some what I'm saying may be a small aspect of a relationship but let me put it to you like this; this man kisses me gently on my forehead each and every time he sees me. Do you know how sensual it is for this man to touch the back of my neck and smile at me? Imagine how special I feel when I answer my telephone and hear him say he was thinking about me; knowing in my heart that he feels like he is missing a bone from his own rib when the two of us are apart. I have a man in my life that knows the smell of my perfume, a man that sees things that remind him of me, a man that knows when I need a hug, a man who is willing to invest himself in my joys and victories as well as my times of sadness and defeats. I never even imagined that it could be like this; that I could actually find a man who would give a fuck about my being happy. *He actually found me.* I know I have personally longed for a man that could love me the way I need and deserve to be loved. I have always been in search of someone who would lift all the boundaries and let me be free to be me ~ the type of love that our souls long for and strong relationships are built on. And then love called...

"Hi Baby"

"Hey Erik, I have been waiting for your call all day. You must have been really busy, huh?"

"Yes I have but you know what they say, all work and no play makes..."

"Baby you could never be dull so don't even go there."

"So what's the plan for tonight? I was thinking we would go hear some spoken word up on Melrose and then maybe get a bite to eat. It's on you. Whatever you want to do is cool."

"Let's just kick back tonight in front of the TV and I'm even going to cook you dinner for a change, maybe even give you a little back massage..."

"You can cook? I'm all in. My last meeting is at 3:30 so I'll be leaving here no later than five o'clock. I'm going to pick Bailey up from school and head your way, okay?"

"I'm going to be stuck until around six o'clock myself so get the key from under the flower pot and let yourself in. I shouldn't be long. See you then"

"I can't wait to see you baby. Be careful"

"You too..."

Maybe it was shit like this that had Florida so content with James; that made her trust that one day things would get better. Maybe they had the magic that it takes to maintain love even when you're sleeping in a rat hole. I know I could sleep in Grand Central Station as long as Erik is sleeping with me. See what I'm saying. So I think I know what Florida and James had to be feeling; something real.   Who am I to knock them…

***

This day has taken what seems like forever to end.   I really need to get to the gym (yeah, since I've been dating Erik I have been going to the gym) but I don't want to be apart from Erik any longer than I have to.   I've actually dropped a good twenty pounds since he and I have been together.   Funny how this man makes me want to be the very best me, you know what I mean. I want to be a better person, a better woman, a better friend, a better mother, a better lover.   He makes me want to be perfect but never faults me for my imperfections.   He respects my mind.   When you're so connected with someone on a mental level, do you know you don't miss the sex.   Really, you don't.   I mean, Erik makes love to me over and over again ~ mentally.   *But I actually do miss the sex part…*

He has really shown me something really special; something I have never experienced before. Being with Erik makes me forget that I am in the middle of a bitter divorce war with Mister's bitch ass. Speaking of Mister, I have been avoiding his call all week and I know I have to call him back but he represents a chapter in my life that I would rather forget. That's hard to do when I have two precious reminders that take me to a place that wasn't so bad, *in the beginning*.

I promised him I would call him back on my way home tonight. Lord knows I need to hold myself together because his punk ass hasn't been to pick up the boys since he was served with divorce papers, so you know he hasn't paid any child support either. *A crazy bitch!* I do wish him and his whore, as well as his screwed up mother, the best of luck but when you're a fucked up individual in all aspects, it's hard to have anything good happen to you. Either way, I will call him when I get to the car this evening.

"Karma, your 3 o'clock is here and waiting for you in the conference room." Hunter announces over the intercom.

"Let them know I will be right in and tell Garrett to meet me in the hallway. Thanks Hunter."

This account with Chamber and Associates is huge for our firm. Over the next three years, our company would profit an estimated three million dollars. I'm ecstatic about our company being selected to head this project. It means some long hours and dedication on the part of our staff but the experience and the pay check will be our vindication.

I really hate late afternoon meetings but today I have no choice. Garrett and I are meeting with the CEO of Chambers to present our full proposal and product launch game plan. Chambers has developed a revolutionary skin care line aimed to promote healthy tanning solutions. The target population: anyone who needs a tan.

"Gentlemen, thank you for taking the time to meet with us today. We hope to be brief and painless. My business partner, Garrett and I have developed the roll out plan for your product which requires your final approval. Garrett has created a presentation that covers all the vital components of the launch. He will be able to answer all your questions at the end of the presentation. Now I will turn things over to Garrett."

"Thank you Karma. If I can turn your attention to the screen…"

Garrett is an excellent presenter. Presenting ideas and gaining buy in was his specialty when we worked together in the hell hole. Nothing has changed. All I see is heads nodding in agreement. At the close of his presentation, no one from the Chambers group has any questions. Damn, we nailed it! This account will definitely put Connors Gregory Partners on the map. We have certainly arrived…

***

"Adam, its Karma returning your call"

"Thank you for getting back to me. I have something I need to talk to you about so when can we get together?

"First of all, I'm paying my lawyer three hundred dollars an hour to talk to you and your lawyer, so why would I set aside time to talk to you for free?"

"Karma, it's important. I would have never called you if it wasn't. It's a matter of life and death. When do you have time?"

"It is important to you Adam, not me. The only free time I have to talk to you is this drive from the office. Other than that your shit out of luck as you should be. I'm raising my kids by myself and shit I'm not going to take time away from them to give to you. Who the fuck are you?"

"I would really rather not discuss this over the phone..."

Talk about déjà vu. I've been here before with this shit about not wanting to talk about something over the phone. Only that time his serious conversation turned out to be more fortifying than anything, at least for me. So I might as well try my luck again, you never know...

"Look Adam, it's been a long day. The only time I can promise you, is right now so if there's something on your mind, you need to let it off."

"Well you remember when I went to the hospital a couple of months ago?"

"Yeah I remember. Get to the point."

"Karma, they found something that wasn't so good."

"What did they find?"

"I don't know how to tell you this…"

"You know what; I don't have time for no dumb shit. Say what you have to say or hang this mutha fucka up!"

"Karma, I'm HIV positive…"

"What did you just say?"

"I'm HIV positive. Karma, I thought it was best if you heard it from me. I have been trying to find a way to tell you this shit for weeks."

"What did you just say?"

"I'm positive and I need you to get checked…"

He can't be telling me this shit over the phone. How fucking heartless and careless! I could jump through this phone and beat his ass! He just told me that he's HIV positive. I know I heard him right. I'm supposed to get tested? What the hell is really going on? Did he *really* just tell me that he's HIV positive and I need to get checked? What the fuck did this mutha fucka just say!

Lord Jesus, I know he just told me that he's HIV positive! Lord, I know I curse too much and Lord I know that I'm married with a boyfriend but Lord, my Father in Heaven, if you spare me this time, I promise you I will make some changes. I will make right some things I know I have been doing wrong. I can't have contracted this deadly disease. My children… What about my children. They need me so much. I'm really all they have other than you Lord. Please spare me this time and I will be different. Lord please have mercy on me…Have mercy on my soul… please Lord…

Chapter Nine: Is There A Problem?

"And the men likewise gave up natural relations with women and were consumed passion for one another, men committing shameless acts with men and receiving in their own persons the due penalty for their error."
Romans 1:27

With good reason, I haven't been able to wrap my head around the idea of the possibilities. I'm angry, but not at Mister. I'm angry at my own ass! I should have never trusted him. I should have never given him enough room in my life to contemplate having unprotected sex with him. What a concept; can't even fuck your own husband these days without putting on a jacket. I would rather be safe than nervous as a mutha fucka trying to wait for these results. Let me tell you, three days can seem like a lifetime when you're waiting for a negative or positive; an innocent or guilty. I can say this, I know how people feel when they're on trial looking at the death penalty, really I do.

I have been beating myself up because I knew that something was different about Mister all along. Remember I mentioned that. He would always need something more. Its one thing for a man to cheat but it was so extreme with Mister. It was like he never got any ass in high school so he was trying to make up for lost time. Everybody knows that when a man has to constantly fuck around, he's trying to ward off something much deeper than that, right? Mister had a bitch for every day of the week ~ horrible, lazy bitches at that. Being straight out of the projects was the only prerequisite. Shit that the average man wouldn't even think about fucking with, he'd actually pay for it. That's what concerns me the most…

I wonder if he has called all of them and told them his bad news. If he did, I wonder if they think his limb dick ass was worth the couple minutes that they spent screwing him. I wonder do they feel like I do ~ you know, like whatever they have gotten from Mister, they actually deserve. This was my husband and everyone around him knew that he was married. When these whores were fucking him they just didn't give a shit because they thought his bitch ass was something that he will never be; a man worth having. He certainly isn't a man worth fucking, take it from me. I think of all the times I could have had a V-8 instead of a nut. With all he has done to me over the years, I don't give a fuck about him or them. I just want to be straight…

After we got married he never satisfied me sexually anyway. I bet he didn't even know that I faked it each and every time. It was like being married gave his ass a pass to bore the shit out of me in the bedroom. I would fake it just to hurry up and get it over with. He would think he was really getting down and I would want him to hurry the fuck up. Once he hit the two minute mark, I knew that it wouldn't be long. Finally, after finding out that he had the fucking audacity to cheat on me, I stopped screwing that ass all together. *As every woman should…* Who wants to get AIDS from one of these assholes?

I thought about cheating on him a million times with a couple of men I met along the way, but I never did. I should have cheated but I didn't. Unless going out to dinner, the movies and enjoying someone else's company is considered cheating. If it is, I cheated the entire marriage. I'm like every other woman, attention from a man is important to me. I've always had more male friends than female friends anyway. For me, it was less of a headache to discuss my personal feelings with my male friends than my female friends. You know sometimes we can give each other some real fucked up advice and know we're bullshitting when we give it…

So many thoughts have been running through my head about the outcome of the test results. I have avoided Erik the entire weekend and he's starting to trip a little. Shit, he should just back the fuck up unless he wants me to tell him what's really on my mind. I decided to spare him the details until I'm sure one way or the other; you know what I'm saying. Why put this man through some unnecessary bullshit if I don't have too?

The smallest victims in this stupid shit are my boys. I could kick Mister's bitch ass just for making me have to worry about their well-being. I know he never gave a fuck about these kids but I always tried to fool myself. I mean a man that loves his kids would never put them at risk like this. I have never wanted this punk bitch to be perfect because I know that his lineage is just too fucked up to think that he would be anywhere near adequate. You know that scientist can trace fucked up all through out your ancestry – did you know that? Yes they certainly can. See you just don't end up fucked up; it's in your pedigree. If you're a fucked up individual like Mister, you come from a long list of fucked up bitches – male and female. Yeah, you don't just happen to be fucked up, it's a family trait; a recessive jean. Sort of like DNA. How could your mother and your father be fucked up and screwed the fuck up and you turn out anything other than fucked and screwed. Just doesn't happen!

The next time I follow a man home to meet his parents, I bet you I will pay close attention to the way they get down as a unit. And if the parents aren't on speaking terms, I will politely excuse myself and exit stage left. Really I will...

I just keep hearing the song 'In the Morning' by the Winans and Anita Baker. You remember the song...

Ain't no need to worry,
what the night is gonna bring,
it'll be all over in the morning.
Troubles come, but they do past,
heartaches, hurts, oh but, they don't last always.
Sometimes we feel pain,
but there are things that we can change, just pray...

I know the Lord has sent an angel to watch over me, you know. Even though I feel undeserving, I know that He's going to protect me in this situation. So I can't keep worrying myself about what the outcome will be. He is my faith when I feel like I am not able, I call on Jesus and he answers. He's still standing next to me. When I feel like I'm not able to go on, the Lord tells me I belong to him so nobody can hurt me...

Matter of fact, let me get myself up out of this bed and take Justin and Kyle to church. I can run this race. This will be over in the morning...

***

I dropped the boys off at school this morning and called in sick today. Shit, I am sick! Been sick all weekend.

I'm at my doctor's office early; helped them open the office this morning. My appointment isn't until 2:30 but there's nothing wrong with being a little early. What is it – about 9 o'clock? At least I'm not going to be late. Plus, Dr. Lark understands my situation and she knows that I'm scared to death.

I haven't told anyone; not even Garrett or Danica. I'm embarrassed to even mention this shit to them. They're both so blunt that they may tell me how foolish I was to even marry Mister in the beginning and I'm not sure I want to hear anything like that right now. What's done is done and it is what it is. Whatever Dr. Lark tells me, I know that I will have to face the shit head on. I really didn't do anything wrong but have sex with my husband anyway. I have always been a fighter so I stay down (I don't have a ounce of punk in me) but this is one battle I would rather not fight. And talk about timing being fucked up...

Finally met someone that I truly respect and he respects me. Erik is a caring man that is not hung up in sex and all that. He is the type of person that you want your daughters to hook up with. I've been tripping on him all weekend because I couldn't tell him something like this. What would I say ~ *Erik by the way Mister's bitch ass is HIV positive and I might be too.* Nope! Don't think that would go over too well. I'm just going to sit here and read *Good Housekeeping* until Dr. Lark calls me in…

"So we have your test results missy and…"

"Is there a problem?"

Dr. Lark is one of the most sought after young, Black, female doctors in the Palos Verdes area. She reminds you of one of your girlfriends. This lady has the perfect beside manner. I trust her with my life. I was actually referred to her by another doctor after having irregular periods for over two years. I would have cycles that would last for weeks. Yes, weeks! She saved my life because I was ready to commit suicide with all that damn bleeding. It was horrible! She immediately diagnosed the problem and I have been good every since.

"Well your results are negative so there's no problem."

"What a relief…"

"What made you think that you had something to worry about?"

"My husband – soon to be ex-husband – came to me and told me he was HIV positive and that I should be checked.   I have been worried all weekend because you never know."

"Yeah, I have seen an increase in married, monogamous women who are HIV positive or who have full blown AIDS. It's not something to play with. When was the last time you had sex with your ex-husband?"

"Dr. Lark it has been some years. I stopped having sex with him many months before we even separated and we have been separated for about eight months now."

"With that said, there isn't any routine follow up that you would need but I do see you're annual pap smear and mammogram is due in the next couple of weeks, so please go ahead and make an appointment so we can get those test out the way too."

"I will stop by the front desk on my way out. Thank you Dr. Lark"

Talk about a load off my mind. Mister has contracted this bullshit without me and he will deal with his bullshit without me. See sometimes in this life we live, we get exactly what we deserve. Lord knows I didn't deserve to be HIV positive when I've done nothing wrong. I respected the vows I took close to six years ago. I honored the union, even when I didn't like the bitch-made asshole. I still didn't break the covenant.

I never asked Mister who, where or how he contracted this shit because I wasn't concerned about all that but now that I know I'm in the clear, I'm curious. Where the hell did his crazy ass get HIV? And what man in this day and time fucks some bitch in the street without extra precautions? Who does that dumb shit! Nobody; that's who! I guess he actually thought he would hurt me by having unprotected sex with men, women, prostitutes and anything else that had a hole, see what I'm saying. He fucked himself this time and how! If he spent less time focusing on me and more time paying attention to these whores in the street, maybe this chapter in his life would have been written a little different, you think? Sometimes it's good to have strings attached, at least that's what I think. However you look at it, the Lord showed me favor and I'm thankful.

I prayed hard over the past couple of days ~ harder than I have ever prayed in my entire life. I was so fearful of how my life could change in an instant. My children were a huge concern. Its one thing to have a stupid ass father, but a stupid ass mother too! That would just be too nutty; more than what they need to endure. I made some promises to the Lord that I *have* to keep because He delivered on His promise to me. There will be some changes in my life, *you'll see...*

Chapter Ten: Did I Do Something Wrong?

"And the rib which the Lord God has taken from the man he made into a woman and brought her to the man."
Genesis 2:22

I've been playing hooky from work for the past four days which is so not like me. I go to work when I can't do anything else. I decided to do some soul searching after what I have been through. Seeing my whole entire life flash before my eyes has been a true eye-opener. I was really scared. This episode really has made me stop and evaluate my life and how I affect the universe. I decided that if I'm going to take control of my life and be the best me that I can be, I need to make sure that I feed my own soul and spirit.

I realize that I have to be complete without the help of anyone else. My happiness is dependent on me and me alone. Life will change without asking permission and I identify with and respect the whole concept of positive change now. Without making changes how would we be able to discover a deeper self and make the desired corrections in our lives. Growth would be impossible. I have a thorough understanding of that age old saying – live each day like it's your last. I made a commitment that if the Lord showed me favor I would make some changes.

Every since the HIV thing, I have been distant from Erik. Yeah, he's tripping out. I think that just having the whole world stop for me to absorb the grave possibilities made the idea of a relationship, you know a man, seem like a unnecessary test of my strength and faith in the Lord. You know what, if the Lord wanted me to have a dick between my legs, He would have certainly put one there. Here I was tripping about not fucking ~ *sorry let me rephrase that* ~ Here I was questioning my self worth because Erik didn't or wasn't trying to have a sexual tryst with me. I guess you can say that I was reacting to what I have become accustom to. So the first thing I'm changing is my mind. At some point my mind and heart have to work in unison rather than as separate entities. I think that point is now.

I have been ducking and dodging Erik long enough. There is a part of me that thinks that I owe him the full story ~ you know the whole thing about the truth being the light. Can he even handle the truth? I guess I will never know if I don't return his calls or see him again…

***

"Karma, you have a call on line two. She says she's your mother-in-law."

"It's my mother-in-law?"

"That's what she said. Do you want to take the call or should I send it to voicemail?"

"Are you sure she said she's my mother-in-law?"

"Karma, that's what she said. What do you want me to do?"

"I'll take it. Thanks Hunter."

Now this has got to be a bad joke. First of all, I have never considered myself to have a mother-in-law. Mister's mother is too much of a miserable piece of shit for me. She can't even love her own grandchildren so you know she can't be a mother-in-law unless they truly come straight from hell. Frankly speaking, the last conversation I had with the bitch was down right ugly so why she would be on my phone is a true mystery. Maybe she wants me to curse her ass out again. And calling me on my job…

This is a place of business and I don't appreciate her calling me on my job with her bullshit. She wanted her son so I gave him to her ~ HIV and all! What could she possibly want with me?

"Karma Bennard, what can I do for you."

"Hello Karma, its Ethel. How have you been?"

"Ethel, I've been happy. What can I do for you?"

"I was calling to see if I could pick up the boys this weekend?"

"No you can not. Is there anything else?"

"Karma, I know we have had a rocky road but I would really like to play a part in the boys' life. They have two sets of grandparents and …"

"Let me tell you something Ethel. First of all they've had two sets of grand-parents way before now. They have managed to do fine without one set because you guys are too fucked up to play a role in the lives of your grand children that are not illegitimate. You're such a pitiful bitch that you can't be a grandmother to my children because of your dislike for me. Trust that the feelings are quite mutual but with that said I would never turn my children over to a woman that I don't trust. I don't want my children exposed to you because, as a human being, you have nothing ~ and I do mean nothing ~ solid to offer a young impressionable mind…"

"As the grandmother, I have a legal right to see the boys."

"You don't have a legal right to a mutha fucking thing! Trust that as long as I feed Justin and Kyle by myself, you pathetic bitches don't have to worry about seeing them. Instead of being on the phone with me, you need to be looking after your son, don't you think."

"That's the reason for my call. Adam wants to see the boys. His health is deteriorating quickly Karma so I'm begging you to please let the boys visit."

"Let me be clear on this; because your son's health is failing due to him running the street with every whore he could find while we were married, I'm supposed to pack my boys up and send them to you and him. He who is HIV positive and not remorseful of any of the shit he has done to me or my children. I'm supposed to now turn the other cheek and send the boys over to love a man that has never had any love for them. A man that has made it evident that he could give a shit. Am I hearing you correctly?"

"That's not what I'm saying and whose to say if he loves them or not. Of course, he loves his children..."

"Well love is an adjective; you know a action word. Your son's actions have shown me that he could give a shit but you know what Ethel, when he stopped giving a shit about my babies, I kept on loving them so fuck you and him!" *Click.*

That was actually stimulating. I got the chance to tell her exactly how I feel. How did she get my work number is the question. I know that Mister isn't crazy (or sick) enough to have his mother call me. She knows I can't stand her ass so why call me. Just call me when he's dead and gone so I can collect on the life insurance.

***

I've come to dread grocery shopping, especially since Erik had started doing this horrifying task. I'm still not able to face him and it's going on some weeks. I did tell him that I would call him when I sort everything out. Reality is I miss him so much. He could never know what he means to me. Especially since I have been running and hiding like I'm in the tenth grade. I kind of feel foolish to be pushing away one of the best men I have ever met. I got to figure some shit (*I mean stuff*) out. I'm seriously trying to find my own destiny. My world is moving so fast now. Deep in my heart the answer is there... The Lord's strength lies within me.

Right now, I'm desperately trying to stick to this list because me and the boys always do our grocery shopping on impulse and when we get home we have a basket full of bull shit and trust me, woman can't live off bull shit alone.

"Mommy, can we get the Captain Crunch?"

"You guys know that stuff has too much sugar and you don't need to get any higher than you already are..."

"What about the Cinnamon Toast Crunch?"

"Look, get the oatmeal like we agreed and let's get out of this isle all together."

"Can we get the pop tarts?"

"I said let's get the oatmeal and don't ask me anymore about something that's not on this list."

Just as Justin and Kyle agree to accept the oatmeal and call it a done deal, I notice this woman walking towards me. I'm going to be honest with you; I never expect to see anyone I know in the grocery store. It just doesn't happen. But today, out of all the full moons, Coreatha is shopping in this grocery store and walking my way. Yeah, Coreatha. I'm so not ready to have any type of dialogue with her ~ Mister is still my husband, *legally*.

"Hi Karma and how have you two been?"

"Hey Coreatha, I've been happy. I have been meaning to call you but I have been busy with the boys and the little league stuff. Girl, I've been busy. How is Adam doing?"

"I guess you haven't talked to him either. He and I have decided to just be friends. I mean, I have a lot of things pending and I just need to get myself together. Really don't have a lot of time right now for a man…"

Wait one minute, isn't this the same bitch that had to have Mister's ass? Now that his ass is burning it's not looking so promising after all. I can't say I'm surprised because Mister should have known that this girl was a second rate whore in the very beginning but he was *fixing* me. Look who got fixed.

"Coreatha, I'm so sorry to hear that you two are not together anymore. I really think you're perfect for each other. So are you okay, I know you must really love him."

"Karma, I have to be honest with you, Adam and this whole HIV thing has me scared to death. The fire is just not there anymore because I can't deal with the whole concept of being with a man who is positive."

"Oh, so you're not? I was under the impression that he got it from you…"

"No! Not at all. I have been tested and so far so good. Why would I hang around and run the risk of getting something from him? And deal with his mother's ignorant ass too – that just doesn't make sense to me."

"Well I can't give you any advice but you need to do what you can live with. I certainly wish you and Adam well. Maybe it will work itself out… The boys are already at the check out so I'll be in touch Coreatha, you take care."

There is a part of me that feels really bad for Mister right now. I mean although I hate that fucka, I don't wish him bad luck or bad health. He should have known though that this girl wasn't really in his corner. See the real thing is Coreatha thought there was some money to be had. They say that the love of money is the root of all evil, so she should be scared and running back and forth to the clinic for testing ~ she earned it. You feel me. I'm not downing the sista though because to be with a man who is HIV positive and counting, has to be hard to do. All I'm saying is that as women, we should consider the damage we're doing when we establish a covenant with the next woman's husband. Not her boyfriend; *her husband*.

In most cases, we should be questioning our own spirit when we "*allow*" these assholes to select which of us he wants to be with. We give them so much power in our lives that we can't even do girls night out without one of us bringing our dude. How pitful is that? But he's not taking sand to the beach. So when he hits the strip clubs and the night spots, your ass is sitting at home hoping that he stops by afterwards. Do you really think he would come by if his tired lines and outdated conversation would get him to first base? Let's be real, some men don't deserve a woman, let alone a good one.

And don't get it twisted, if he does it *with* you; I guarantee, he won't think twice about doing it *to* you. I don't want to preach, so all I have to say is be careful how you get your man…

Personally, I think if I was with someone and he came down with this deadly shit, I would be down for him until the end. But a bitch ass man like Mister is always going to be alone and will probably die alone because I'm certainly not the one to be running to his rescue. Fuck Mister!

***

Tonight is the night for me to talk with Erik. I hope he's still feeling the same way about me. You know I dealt him a pretty hard blow by not calling and not giving any explanation for my behavior. I don't like being alone but I needed some space to get my head around what was going on. I really don't have a long speech or anything planned to say ~ I'm just going to try like hell to keep the shit one hundred and hope that this man will accept that I was confused and didn't know what I was doing and frankly, didn't want to get him involved in all the drama.

- 139 -

A car door just slammed so it must be Erik. Now isn't this some brand new shit, he's on time. He has never been on time. I'm surprisingly impressed. He's either eager to see me or he's ready to give me a good piece of his mind. Either way, it's finally time to have this conversation. He needs to know that there is nothing wrong with us – as a couple. I'm not even sure we're a couple; we really haven't talked about it. The way I understand it these days, you're actually dating until you have "the conversation" about being exclusive. I don't think I ever had the conversation, even with Mister. We just took shit at face value – if I spend all my spare time with you, we're a couple. All these rules in dating, shit I have enough on my plate without making sure I don't break a fucking rule...

That's the door bell and I'm really nervous because how do I even start this conversation off. I know he deserves to know the truth even though my test results were negative. I sure don't want to build a relationship on a lie so I'm just going to open the door and get this shit (*I mean stuff*) off my chest.

"Karma, I'm so glad to see you. Can I have a hug?"

"You certainly can. I'm glad to see you too. Been missing you something terrible…"

"Did I do something wrong? If I did I apologize and I want the chance to make it right. Please accept my apology."

"Erik, if you let me go for a minute I will tell you what has been the problem. See it's like this; Adam called me and told me that he is HIV positive and I had to be tested. I was so nervous that I couldn't think straight and the three day wait didn't help at all. I didn't want to bring you all that unnecessary chaos and drama but I now realize that I should have told you rather than push you away. There was nothing you did wrong accept meet a crazy woman – me! So really, I owe you an apology."

"You are the most intriguing woman that I have met and I appreciate you being considerate of keeping our thing drama free, but I will be supportive of whatever you need to do Karma because that's what friends are for."

"So we're just friends?" I ask out of curiosity.

"You are so much more than a friend. I have managed to fall in love with everything about you. I know you have the divorce and all so I have tried to allow you to do what you need to do for you and your kids but Karma you mean so much to me that I can't even put it into words."

"I feel the same exact way. I have never met a man like you – that I could actually be friends with and trust with my dreams. I think you are an amazing man Erik and I'm blessed to have you in my life."

Now I have to say I sincerely hooked that up. Funny how things turn out perfect when you shoot from the hip. There have been times when I've rehearsed something I had to say in my mirror so that I wouldn't leave a word out and as soon as it comes time to tell the person, the shit goes all fucked up ~ *let me rephrase that* ~ things go awry and nothing comes out right. I really have to stop this damn cursing…

"Karma, would I be prying to ask the results of your test?"

"Oh I thought I told you that my results came back negative and I'm in the clear because I had stopped being intimate with Adam at least a year before we decided to divorce; can give yourself to a man you can't trust. Are at least that's the way I have always looked at it."

"A year? How did you guys manage that?"

"It's a lot easier than you think once the fire, that initial spark, is gone. I stopped even thinking of him in a sexual way so it was easy for me. And with good reason. Where would I be today had I kept the blinders on?"

"Do you think of me in a sexual way Karma?"

"Do you even have to ask a silly question like that? I have a great idea, why don't you follow me and see for yourself..."

I'm really not one to kiss and tell so this is where this chapter ends. I will say this; he has me grinning like its money that I'm winning. This was a session to remember; some shit that resembled soft porn, I kid you not. Off the hook, over the top, the real shit! I have been to the mountain top. All I can say is hallelujah! *Of course we used a condom; I always love responsibly...*

Chapter Eleven: Do I Look Crazy?

"Blessed shall you be when you come in, and blessed
shall you be when you go out."
Deuteronomy 28:7

I really think that people in general want to see
other people do bad, sort of like crawfish in a bucket;
every time one tries to get out another one pulls him
back in. I know from experience to be careful who you
make a friend. After all the trials and tribulations that
have occurred in my life lately, I have selection criteria
for that ass ~ especially if a person is hanging around
trying to be my friend. It takes a very special person to
be a friend, not to mention a good friend. Every time I
have tried to be a friend, someone ends up mad at me.
Normally its because I have loaned them money and
they always get mad when its time to pay it back. Shit,
I'm the one who should be mad because I have to ask
for money that they know they owe me. I just don't
understand why people think I should give them my
money ~ if it's not worth working for, then it's not

worth having. Don't get me started. That's a different book...

It's like this, every since Garrett and I started the company all the non-believers have decided to get on the band wagon after they're reading about our company in Enterprise, the Times, Newsweek, Essence – shit we even got an honorable mention on Oprah. For us, we made it...

I get tons of resumes and notes from people in my old neighborhood wanting to be a part of what they thought would be a long shot. Some of my childhood friends that never went to class in high school now want to work for Connors Gregory Partners. We're in desperate need of an office manager and I would love to employ someone that really needs the income.

Unfortunately, the majority of the people from my old neighborhood got caught up in drugs and alcohol; you know all the dumb shit that makes for a fucked up life. I'm trying to stop cursing but there's no way to rephrase the real. Every since high school their lives have been completely screwed but I'm suppose to hire one of them to manage my office because my father told them I would. Overlook all the qualified applicants to hire someone who has no experience and a light weight drug addiction. Don't think so. How can a person manage anything if they can't manage themselves? And my daddy needs to stop sidelining and hiring people on the down low; I know he means well but damn at least let them have ninety days sober before you hire them…

Boy am I glad that my parents taught me to believe in myself. With a little determination and a little passion, not to mention some self confidence, you have the perfect recipe for a successful life. Luckily for me, I have been winning my entire life and a minor set back like divorce can't derail what I've already accomplished. A person has to believe in themselves and God. Yeah, God…

I always knew that the Lord's plan supersedes any plan that I make for myself. Plus the Lord plans big! All these little bitty ass plans I have are nothing compared to what He has in store for me. Don't get it twisted though, when He makes plans for us – we got to follow the plan. Don't be running off thinking you got it because you don't. Thinking everything is under control is how we get into the biggest mess. Since I have been going through the shit (*I mean stuff*) with Mister, I learned to let go and really let God. I have learned that in my personal and business life and the Lord has never failed me.

Being back with Erik has been good. You know we have been doing that thing every day and it only gets better. All jokes aside, this man is like the energizer bunny – he just keeps going and going and going... Do you know that he had the nerve to tell me that I can't be saved by the bell? He actually has me sitting at my desk day dreaming and drawing karma sutra diagrams, no joke.

With all that said, the boys love having Bailey around and they simply adore Erik. I got to admit that anytime it gets this good something goes foul. Don't get me wrong, it hasn't been this good in a decade or so. Even then it wasn't this good. So when it gets close to this good, some thing always goes way fucked up. I guess I plant things in my mind to call on later, like the tennis bracelet that was on Erik's dresser the very first time I visited his house. Remember his phone never stopped vibrating. Well I should have said something then but I was just tripping off of the physical attraction in the beginning and could have gave a fuck who that was calling. I was there with him and she's calling on the phone and being ignored at that. Who cares? Let me answer that – *now I do*. I should have asked some questions in the beginning so that I wouldn't seem like a crazy bitch going back eight months to ask some dumb shit now. Don't get me wrong, Erik is cool but I think he would probably wonder why it's important in the here and now. You're probably wondering the same thing. Let me tell you, it's important because I'm giving him ass on a regular, consistent basis now. That's why. I want to know if this psycho bitch (*I mean tramp*) is still calling him and all times of night too. And who the hell is she ~ why all the secrets? I'm paranoid beyond belief because what we have is a good thing and I surely don't want someone to come along and ruin it all. Remember Erik was up calling me at three in the morning – I thought it was a booty call – so why can't he still be making booty calls and house calls. He's the Reverend Good Doctor for real and, yes he does make house calls, I'm a witness and a believer…

***

I have to take my daddy to the doctor today. All I can say is wow! Have you ever just wanted to scream to the top of your lungs? I do all the time these days. The only thing keeping me from screaming now is the fact that I don't think anyone would hear me. That's for real. I have been suffering silently for over a year. I'm thankful that my daddy is still eating plates of food; hard core soul food at that.

Today he's different though. First of all, he's quiet. Not him at all. I'm going to let it go because everyone needs some down time to get into their own head. He has a look in his eyes that is different. I know he's on morphine but today its not the morphine high that I see. I see a calm, rested man who in all aspects has resolved all his earthly concerns. It's a hard realization for me but at least the Lord gave me what I can handle. I don't think I could see my daddy be one hundred pounds and hooked up to machines and ventilators. I would lose my mind! I understand that he may have fought as long as he could and he's done with this now. I know that and I see that in him. Yeah, I'm dying on the inside because I don't care how much preparing you do, you're never ready for this. If I cry right now I will only make him worry about me. Can you get ready for that shit? He will worry about me, when he has cancer and should be worrying about only himself.

They call us immediately into the office to see the doctor. Daddy is a hot mess, out here waving like he's running for president or something. The nurses always tell me that he's too much ~ who knows what the they mean by that? I always thought he was just enough but I can't even begin to imagine what Daddy has said or done to these nurses over the years, so I elect not to ask.

"So Mr. Bennard, how is everything going?"

"It's rough man. I'm still among the living so that's a good thing but hell living like this is not for me…"

"What do you mean?"

"Ever had cancer Doc?"

"No, I can't say I have."

"Well when you get it you will know exactly what I mean. Not wishing you no bad luck but everything you read in them books of yours can't compare to what this is really like."

"Is there anything I can do Mr. Bennard to make this better?"

"Funny you should ask Doc. There is something you can do. Let's me and you change places and you battle cancer and I will write everything you say down. I'll send you home to die and I will go home and play with my grandsons. See my wife and my children. I'll be back here tomorrow at the same time and wonder if you made it through the night."

"Mr. Bennard I sympathize with you and your family and my heart goes out to you and them. Miracles happen every day so don't give up on yourself."

"Look here boy, what do you know about giving up on yourself? When you're over seventy and a Black man in White America, you learn real quickly not to give up. Let me explain something to you. When you were attending your fancy medical school, I was already in my third career. I raised my kids and my brother's kids. I have suffered the indignities of this racist society long before you was even born son. The attitude of the White man has always been that of disgust when it came to Black men, see that's nothing new. Started when you all felt you had to protect your women from the big bad Black man. That's when all this stuff started young man. Every since, you all thought you would have to take care of a Black man and give him a free ride. I want you to know I never was able to ride in this life for free and I've never asked for a favor from anybody. I stood up and took care of my family and probably some of your family. I never complained. So when you say don't give up – you really don't know anything about the miles I've walked and if I would have been a quitter, you all would have killed me long ago. So watch your mouth young man because you don't want to have to walk a mile in my moccasins."

Needless to say, the doctor is drawn to tears now. Daddy had a lot of shit he needed to say I guess. The doctor must have hit a cord for real with that give up shit so Daddy gave it to him. I'm surprised it wasn't worse. He got it off his chest and that's all that really matters.

On the ride home, he and I spark a conversation and he shares all the things that have been heavy on his heart. It was reassuring for me to know that he's okay. I mean really okay with his circumstances. I guess it was my own personal fear that made me think that a man of his caliber would be afraid of a little thing like death. He's not. Thank God that he is who he is.

With my Daddy, everything is going to be alright. I'm confident that he's going to be alright...

***

Oddly enough Erik has been taking the boys over to see Mister. I'm not tripping, they can see him everyday of the week but they're not spending a night. Looks like he is in the last stage of his disease and everyone is calling me. Do you know the judge even postponed signing our divorce decree for three months. I have never heard of some shit so ridiculous. I'm still in need of a divorce and now more than ever. Let his ass marry Coreatha ~ oh that's right ~ she left his ass when she realized that he was a complete asshole with AIDS.

Reality is, if Erik hadn't agreed to take Kyle and Justin to see him, they would have never seen him again. I mean that from the bottom of my heart. See Mister is a dirty bastard that stopped paying child support, stopped picking them up for visits and the whole nine yards when he realized that I may be having a life of my own every other weekend. Let's not forget the fact that whenever he has a funky whore, my boys take a back seat to his bullshit with a bitch. Believe it or not, I had stopped cursing. Really I did until right now. The thought of Mister having my children around his diseased ass after a bitch leaves him high and dry makes me want to go off. I wouldn't feel this way had he stayed connected to the boys while his bitch was around and frankly, before he came down with AIDS. Why now are my children important?

I'm not even going to beat a dead horse; Erik is in control of the whole Mister situation so I don't even have to deal with the shit at all. He has been a real blessing to Justin and Kyle. I mean being a real support to them in this ordeal with their dad. Bailey and I have become close friends too. While they're gone to visit with Mister, she and I go shopping, to the day spa, out to lunch. I love my boys but having a daughter is something wonderful. I have turned Bailey into a true princess. I think this is what life was supposed to be all the time. I'm good...

"Hey little men, you're back from your dad's..."

"Yes mommy, he said to tell you 'hello' and he will call you next week."

"He did. Erik what does he want with me? Do you know?"

"He just wants to talk to you Karma. You know he's there by himself and his mother is doing the very best she can do but she's can't take care of him. I think he was thinking that maybe he could move into the pool house so that he can be close to Justin and Kyle."

"What pool house; my pool house?"

"Yeah, move back here so that he can be around his kids…"

"My kids? He never wanted to be around them before and to move into my pool house means he would have to be around me and I don't want his ass dying here."

"Karma, you shouldn't say that. I mean you need to let some stuff go beautiful and do what you need to do for your children's father."

"Whose bright idea was it for him to move in my pool house? And does he know that we're in the mist of a divorce because we're two mutha fuckas who don't want to be around each other…"

"It was actually my suggestion. I know I should have mentioned it to you before I spoke to him but it seems like the only logical thing to do."

"So Erik, it seems logical for me to move my ex-husband into my pool house and take care of him because he has AIDS. So it's logical for me to continue to get sucked into his bullshit. That's logical to you? Don't even answer that because I see he has brain washed your ass too."

"It's really not about all of that. It's about your sons and their being able to be with their father during his last days. I mean it is only obvious that he's not going to be here another six months and the time he has with them is limited. So you would have to unselfishly agree to allow him to live in your pool house and pay you a little rent so that he can..."

"He has another child, remember? Another one that he claims to love to death, so go live in that bitch's fucking pool house. Do you think I'm going to allow this man to fuck over me in life and in death ~ *do I look crazy?*"

"Karma, would you just give it some thought. I mean I agreed to help his mom out by stopping by and handling some of the things around his apartment. Help him change clothes and..."

"Now this is really fucking amazing – you two are best friends now. Well I'll be a monkey's uncle."

"Okay, I'm not going to mention it anymore but do think about it baby. Get some of that anger off your chest because what happened in the past doesn't even matter anymore."

Erik is crazy too. Men always think you're stupid. In any given situation they think a woman should be a slave and get beat down before she decides its time to stand up. With all the shit I have told him this man has done to me over the years, it doesn't seem feasible for Mister to be in the same zip code with me; let alone my house. I don't want him in the same time zone with me so you know how I'm feeling about him being a short walk across the pool. If he's that sick let him go to a convalescent home. *Mister is not my problem.* He is not even a concern of mine. And Erik is going to mess around with all these bright ideas and he's going to be away from me too. How could he come up with something so dumb? Yeah he's part of the coalition to keep a woman subservient to some low down ass man, that's how he dreamed that shit up.

People always think because you wear a smile that you're crazy. Well I got news for both of them, neither one of them better mess with me or they will both be out there. *I must look crazy…*

Chapter Twelve: Did You Forget About Me?

"If you afflict them, and they cry out to me, I will surely hear their cry..."
Exodus 23:23

I have to be honest, Erik is truly an angel sent from Heaven. I never ever dreamed that I would actually love a man like this. For my angel, I would stop breathing if my life was possible without air. He goes out of his way for me and my children and that means more than words can convey. With what I have been through with Mister and losing the ability to love, right now angels and devils look alike to me. That's for real.

Erik has stepped into my life and changed my attitude towards the whole "love" thing but life has disappointed me in this category so why risk myself again. With all that I have told him about my rocky marriage, I don't see how he can now be the surrogate care giver for Mister. To knowing take care of this man that he knows have dealt nothing but heartbreak and disappointment to me and my boys, is crazy to me. I guess the choice is his and you know he's a Christian. Funny how Christianity goes out of the picture when we're here getting our groove on. Oh yeah, we're sexing at least a couple of times a week these days and church boys really know how to make you say "Amen". Yes, we both know better but I'm a work in progress and some habits take a little longer to break; especially when you have been on a long drought.

Meanwhile, when he's not here with me and the kids; he's with Mister and Ethel helping with whatever needs to be done. I don't know if I should applaud his crazy behavior or be pissed at him. You know what I mean. It's just way beyond what my *boyfriend* should be doing for my *ex-husband*. Mister is now my ex-husband, *legally*. He finally decided that rather than take time out of his suffering to make me miserable, that he owed it to Justin and Kyle to man up and give them what is rightfully theirs. I was able to retain ownership of our family residence and our vacation home in Myrtle Beach as well as legal custody of my children. But on the other hand, Mister was ripped to shreds downtown playing with that man in that black robe. He repeatedly tried to make it seem like there was no money to divide and was hiding his assets. So in the end he owes me over two-hundred thousand dollars for my boys' college fund. He owes my boys a car valued at no less than thirty thousand once they get their licenses. And he also owes my attorneys a good fifty thousand. I guess the judge should have asked him did he want starch too ~ it's called the cleaners.

I am in no way celebrating the destruction of the family unit but I believe that everyone gets what they deserve. I can't tell you how devoted I was to my marriage and how bad I wanted it to work out, only for that fool to show his ass. *Excuse my French.* No, I don't hate Adam but I certainly won't allow him to spit on me on his way out. He has done enough over the period that we were married to last a lifetime so why would I go running to his death bed now. I'm just not that kind of a person. Although the Lord is working miracles in my life and blessing me on a daily basis, He didn't say be no fool.

So follow this if you can. My new boyfriend is taking care of my ex-husband whose dying of AIDS because my sons need their father to die with dignity and he has nobody but *his momma*... Is that not crazy?

***

"Ms. Bennard, something strange has happened."

"What is that?"

"After going over your father's most recent test results, I had the nurse call you right away. We tested him several times because we had to be sure that what we were seeing wasn't a lab mistake. After all the results were in and reviewed by our team, it looks like your Dad's cancer has gone into full remission. The mass that we originally saw has decreased from the size of say a watermelon to the size of an apple."

"What does that mean?"

"That means that when your Dad says he feels fine, he actually does. He should see an increase in energy and have the ability to walk on his own. We're not saying go out and do what he use to but he should surely see an increase activities. We have never seen anything like this and we would like to continue to monitor his health and he should continue to take his meds but…"

"You know what Doctor, I have prayed harder for my father than I have ever prayed for myself. Remember when you said that miracles happen? Well my father is proof that the Lord hears prayers and sends down miracles to those who are deserving of a blessing."

"You're absolutely right Karma, may I call you Karma?"

"Yes. You certainly can."

"I too believe in miracles and blessings and the scripture for that matter. Can I see your father back here in about two weeks?"

"He will be here with bells on."

"Be sure to stop at the front desk and make an appointment. Take care."

"Thank you Doctor. See you in two weeks."

Now get a load of that! You know I'm in seventh heaven after getting this news. I can hardly get to my car without skipping; damn near running out of joy. I have to go by and tell my mom and dad; can't forget to call my brother and my cousin. Got to tell Erik, Danica and Garrett too! Shit this is cause for a celebration so dinner is on me…

***

Erik and I are getting together this evening after what seems like a lifetime of being apart. Taking care of Mister has become a full time profession. I guess after all is said and done, taking my man is Mister's way of saying "gotcha" in the ninth inning. I can't stand him!

I can't knock Erik for doing what he thinks is appropriate; or what his heart has led him to do. But my heart is leading me a totally different way. I'm not even going to visit because I was in the same household with Mister and we didn't visit then. Matter of fact, we didn't even speak half the time. So there's no need to race to his bedside now ~ plus I'm *officially* the ex-wife; *legally*. One thing I'm not doing is tripping off his plight.

You know what I think. I think had Mister married me with the right intentions and took our vows a little more seriously; especially the part about honoring the union, he would be as healthy as an ox right now. Don't get me wrong, I did my share of bad deeds myself but it was only after Mister started running around with different women *or whatever.* I don't blame the women because I wasn't married to them; I was married to him.

I'm just shocked at Erik's commitment to helping Mister. He has been taking the boys to visit a couple of times a week. He has been explaining in detail about being true to one woman ~ and that finding a wife is a good thing. He's really a compassionate man and I guess having a Christian heart goes a lot further than having venom for someone (especially because they just so happen to have met a person before you did).

I miss the closeness that we had because he wants to discuss Mister and his bitch-ass momma (Lord forgive me ~ I take that back) but I don't want to hear any updates on his health, his life or his mutha f**king momma! See I've changed. I don't curse as much. Some of this just doesn't feel fair ~ to me, to my children and what about me? In all of this, did everyone forget about me?

I hope that Erik arrives on time because my patience this evening is short and I'm not feeling it. We're meeting at my favorite restaurant and he says he has a surprise for me. I hope its Frankie Beverly concert tickets because their in town next week and I really want to go. I love Frankie Beverly and Maze.

Try to see my side of this. I really feel like Mister's final performance is just to mess up my life. I mean, at this point he has taken my man from me; not to mention my children. They are all rallying around him and I'm here alone (even Bailey is going to visit these days). Now I don't expect people to take sides but it would be nice if someone would remember that Mister brought all of this on himself.

Frankly, I'm confused. I don't understand Erik's approach to this whole situation ~ my situation that is really none of his business. How did they become so close that he feels compelled to be the caregiver for Mister anyway? I really want some answers and I don't want to hear the sweet shit (*I mean stuff*) that he comes up with. I don't want to hear anything to pacify my heart! I want the real...

"Hey Karma, give me some sugar girl."

"Hey yourself. I was starting to think that you weren't going to make it."

"Never that baby. Did you order already?"

"No I haven't. How are you doing Erik? I never see you anymore and I'm pissed to say the least. Then when I do see you it's obvious that you're tired. Have you been sleeping over at Adam's because I've been calling your house?"

"Karma, I have been busy at work and running myself raggedy trying to help Ethel but I'm cool..."

"I miss you a lot Erik, really I do. *Did you forget about me?*"

"Baby, you know that I haven't forgotten about you but you know what I'm up against. I understand your position on the entire topic and I won't even go there tonight Karma. I don't even think I told you I love you lately but you know I do…"

"For all I know you love Adam. And you know what Erik; I don't want to seem psycho or anything but when I first came to your house there was a tennis bracelet that was on your dresser. I never asked, and I probably shouldn't now, but who did it belong to?"

"What? I'm not sure I know what you're asking?"

Yeah, I bet he's not sure. He's buying some time for a response, that's all. Yeah, let it roll around in his head for a minute so he can think of what to say next. I know he has some woman on the side ~ shit I may be the woman on the side these days. Either way, he needs to tell me something. I know I should have asked months ago but timing is everything and honestly, I wasn't feeling insecure back then. I am now and I want him to reassure me that there's no one else ~ I mean other than Mister's crazy butt (*I meant to say crazy mutha fucking ass*).

"You want to talk about that now?"

"What time is better than the present Erik? I mean I asked the question for a reason so go ahead and tell me something…"

"Let me start by saying that there is no one that means more to me than you. Let's be clear on that one thing. I have never had a reason to hide anything from you when it has come to another woman. But some of my reason for asking you here tonight is to come clean on some shit that's probably going to blow your mind. I would rather not tell you what I have to say in a crowded restaurant so let's go to my place after dinner and talk…"

Now I wasn't looking for anything mind blowing. Matter of fact I would have accepted some sweet shit but mind blowing – I'm not really feeling that right now. What the hell could he be getting ready to hit me with? Here we go again…

***

I still say there is something real gay about Erik's house. Maybe gay is not the right term for it but you know what I mean. There's nothing out of place and then again there's that jasmine in the air. He'd better talk quick because I'll be in here snoring soon. It's just that relaxing. Plus with all the turmoil that I have had in my life recently, how much more can I tolerate?

"You want a drink Karma?"

"No, I'm cool."

"Well I need one and you probably will need one yourself. So I'm going to make you one anyway." He says with a laugh.

You know serious shit is never funny to me. I take that back. I know from experience that you have to sometimes laugh to keep from going dead off, you know what I mean. Through all the trials and tribulations, crooks and turns, forks in the road and everything in between, I have had to keep my sense of humor throughout this journey called life. Put it to you like this, Erik better hope I can find humor in whatever he's about to tell me because this could certainly be the straw…

"Karma, I love you so much…"

"Yeah, I love you too…"

"Baby hear me out and don't interrupt me because I got to tell you this shit… You know when I first hired your agency; I knew exactly who *you* were. I had confidence in your ability and the skills of your firm. Really I did. When I met you it was an instant attraction. I know I fell in love with you when I first saw you. No bullshit. But I haven't been totally honest about all of that…"

Well I knew that the sugar-coated bullshit was coming. Now my heart is pounding because I know it's probably worse than I thought. He is gay! I just knew it! There's no way his house looks like this and he's not! Worse than that he probably has also gotten AIDS from Mister and now he's going to be on life support too. You know what; my life is ruined. I was busy doing me when I got with this man ~ I should have kept doing what I had been doing. Not messing with any of them. Like I said angels and devils all look alike to me. But I'm all ears because I'm going to blow up the spot when he tells me some dumb shit and I know its coming...

"When my brother was killed I took on the responsibility of raising Bailey because I wanted to give her a good home. Her mother has been in and out of rehab but I have never denied her the right to see her daughter. One day she comes to me and she tells me that Bailey may not be my brother's daughter after all and that this other guy she was messing with wanted to take a DNA test. Well at that point it didn't matter, she was already my daughter or niece; however you want to look at it. We all agreed that the best thing for Bailey would be to take the test. The results come back and prove that my brother couldn't be Bailey's father; the other guy is. So the dude and I start trying to figure out a way for her to meet her family. That's where you come in Karma... Please hear me out... That's when Adam tells me to give you a call about the launch. Karma when I met you I knew he had to be fucking crazy! I just couldn't understand how a man could not appreciate having a woman like you. Initially I was supposed to just have Bailey meet Kyle and Justin but Karma, I was so into you. I can look at you and tell you're pissed right now but please baby, understand that I would have walked through hell in a gasoline jumpsuit just to be with you... The whole AIDS thing was a shock for me... And the bracelet, it was your anniversary present that Adam never gave to you because of what went down. He wanted me to give it to you when we got together that night but I couldn't... When my phone was ringing all night it was Adam wanting to know what happened... After all was said and done, I think he was a little upset that I was with

you and feeling you and wanting to marry you...
I know you probably hate me now and I want
you to know that I never meant to hurt you. The
shit just got so far out of hand. I do love you..."

Wait one damn minute. Let me get this shit
straight. Bailey is Mister's daughter and Erik is her
adopted father, uncle, what? Now this shit is confusing
– Bailey is Kyle and Justin's sister and Mister's ass is
this little girl's father that Erik is raising. Wow... Talk
about some twisted shit! I wonder can this mutha fucka
make his head spin completely around. I feel like I'm in
the middle of a Stephen King movie or something. I
can't help but to laugh because this shit is just too crazy
for a sista like me. Talk about some way out shit!

"Karma, I wanted to break it down to you way
before now but I didn't know how and I was
afraid that I would lose you. You're such a huge
part of me and I can't be without you..."

"You know what Erik, I'm not even mad. This is actually funny to me because I said to myself in the beginning that Adam was putting some strange man up to calling me with some bullshit. I said that in my head from the very start. So the jokes on me…"

"It was never a joke. And Karma, I'm sorry I didn't come clean long before now but baby you can't deny what we feel for each other. You can't just throw in the towel. There's too many emotions involved. Adam and I had a long conversation and I told him that I need to tell you because I planned on asking you to marry me tonight. That was my surprise. He gave his approval…"

"You must be joking! Who needs Adam's approval for anything? You got to be fucking bullshitting me! You know what; I don't know if I should hate your ass right now or love you.

How the hell were you able to keep all this shit a secret… All the lies, deceit and constantly cover up. Takes a man with a lot of bitch in him to do all of that… Like I said, I knew something wasn't right when you first called my house. I knew Adam was behind some crazy shit. You know what, I don't even care how you kept it a secret just let me get my purse and get out your house!"

It's time for me and Mister to have some dialogue. And he better hope I don't pull the plug on his ass. Erik is not innocent either – underhanded, low down ass. Willing to go through all this shit for… Well I don't know what for. But his ass is on my shit list; at least for now. Sadly enough, I want to run back into his house and give him a hug (maybe even give him some) but my pride… You know pride is over rated. *I told you angels and devils look alike…*

Chapter Thirteen: Is This The End?

"He who testifies to these things says, 'Surely I am coming soon.' Amen. Come Lord Jesus!"
Revelation 22:20

At least my Daddy is doing better. He's not in the clear; cancer just doesn't work like that but he's feeling good and looks better too. He's in remission and outside everyday promising the entire neighborhood jobs at my agency. I believe in miracles and he's proof that they actually happen. Just pray...

I haven't spoken to Erik. You know he's a trip with all that drama – *like a woman*. That's just too feminine for me; you know keeping a secret with Mister. Actually the truth is, I have been going crazy because I want to be with him so bad. But that stuff was too much for me to handle and he'll know I'm a fool for love if I accept that. You know some good comes out of all this ~ I have learned to share what's in my heart and more importantly, I have a renewed confidence in love. Yeah, L-O-V-E! I know that if a person opens their heart and mind to being in love ~ love will come. Sort of like Erik came to me.

I have to say that I believe every word that he said a couple of weeks ago. There's so much going on beyond my four walls though. I trust Erik, I believe that he was doing what he thought was best for me and my boys. I just have to share what's in my heart, you know... Just focus on the two of us... That's not too much to ask.

It's really about being mature; about being brave. I know I'm emotional. I don't know what to do; don't know what's left to prove. I can't decide. Maybe I will drop a note or card in the mail to Erik today just to let him know he's still on my mind...

To do that would be admitting that even I need someone and that there's a great possibility that I'm not made of stone. I would have to admit to not only Erik, but to myself, that it's okay to be vulnerable, connected, attached and he would have to understand those feelings without holding it against me or thinking I'm weak. What a hard call but that's where my head is at now.

One thing I do know I'm marching right up to see Mister today. If the Lord gives me the ability to breathe today, I will see him and how!

***

Black people always put sick people in the living room. I wonder why that is? Seems like someone that's sick, terminally ill, would rather be in the privacy of a bedroom or something. But to be the first thing that all visitors see when they walk through the door, that's just plain country. And it's cold blooded for the sick person.

Yeah, Mister is lying in a hospital bed dead, smack in the center of the living room. *Country...* He actually looks better than what I imagined, just a little better. Seeing him like this is hard, even for me. I would have never wished this on him. Maybe if I would have been different, things would have turned out different for all involved. I'm in no way blaming myself for his misfortune because he formed his own journey. Here is where it ends.

"Karma, I never thought I would see you again."

"Well you almost didn't but something touched my heart today and told me to come see you. You know I still don't like you and this doesn't change anything…"

"There you go with all those jokes."

"Who's joking?"

"You look good…"

"Always have and you look better than I remember."

"You're still crazy girl…"

"Yeah, and you're still ugly so we're even. So how's life treating you?"

"If the oxygen machine isn't a dead giveaway, I guess I'm doing pretty well."

"So you mean if I turn this button right here, it will be curtains for you…"

"Instantly…"

"Good! So this should be painless, at least for me."

"Karma, I'm glad you came by. You know I owe you an apology for so many things that I don't even know where to start. You tried to be a good wife and mother but I wouldn't let you. You're a good woman and a queen in all rights and I'm sorry for everything, Karma. You have done a great job with the boys and I'm sorry for the position my foolishness has put you in… Karma, I never stopped loving you…"

I came over here to curse him out (as cold as that may sound), not to hear confessions of love and how great I am. I wanted to tell him how messed up he is as a person and how he messed up the perfect life that I had planned. I wanted to hate him right now but what purpose would that really serve; seems like he's hating himself enough for both of us. I guess there is a part of me that will always love him too ~ wow! Never thought I would say something like that but it's my reality.

Maybe I have been looking at things all wrong. If it wasn't for Adam, I would never have met and fallen in love with Erik. Just maybe in the final hour, Adam decided that he would help me find a man that is suitable for a woman like me, you think? It could have just been his way to make right all the wrongs that he committed during our marriage.

"Adam, don't worry about me and the boys, we'll be fine. You know I came over here to continue to hate you all the way to the grave, maybe even rub your nose in your situation, but luckily for you, a light came on because I have a special place for you in my heart. I'm thankful that you found the perfect man for me – Never thought I would be accepting referrals from you but you sent me a good one."

"Erik is the kind of man that I want my sons to grow into. I think he has a lot to offer you and them. He's the kind of man I wanted to be but never could… He's a good man Karma, don't pass him up…" he says as his voice fades.

If this is what I think it is – it was peaceful. *Is this the end?* Mister ~ I mean Adam ~ looks like he just fell off to sleep. I just hope people don't think I killed him; all I need is for everyone to start calling me the Black Widow. I can't say it's not ironic that he would take his final breath with me. I am so glad I came here today. There has been enough anger and bitterness in my life so I needed to close the final chapter between the two of us. Who knows, he may have been just hanging on waiting for me to show up so he could apologize. I think I sought protection through judgment but the Lord sent angels here once I walked in the door. Adam is at peace. So am I…

***

"Hello, Erik. It's Karma…"

"I'm glad to hear your voice. Girl I'm going crazy without you…"

"I'm calling to tell you that Adam passed away today…"

"Yeah, I know. I heard. Are you okay?"

"I'm fine…"

"Are you at home?"

"Yes, I am…"

"Well, I'm on my way. I will see you in about twenty minutes…"

That old saying that every cloud has a silver lining is very true. Throughout all the chaos, all the confusion; the illness, sickness, heart ache – all of that. I'm doing fine. Better than most actually. The Lord has worked miracles in every aspect of my life. You see I'm not cursing as much anymore. I have a great man who loves me and my children which only confirms that there is life after divorce. My sons have a sister that they adore. My business is booming. I'm blessed. What else could I ask for?

I can attest to the fact that I have grown in ways I never even imagined. I can honestly say that it doesn't hurt now. I can understand that some people will come into my life and they don't mean me any good. The beauty in this is I can now see people for who they really are, without all the other stuff that comes with it. I think the Lord has put me through it to make me bigger and better ~ sort of like new and improved.

I know some of my closest friends are really going to trip out when I tell them the story – *the whole story*. I know that if the Lord isn't judging me for all the mistakes I've made ~ and those that I'm sure to make ~ then I would be not only crazy but lonely too, to let Erik walk out of my life.

I guess Mister ~ I mean Adam ~ even had some say so in my life on his death bed; still trying to control me on the sly. He still didn't deserve to have any input but this time I'm taking his word for it. I can finally trust him to be honest and we are in agreement about Erik…

You see, every story has a couple of sides. I really don't know who infected Adam but he paid the ultimate cost for his deceit; his story really has nothing to do with me, as much as people try to say it does. There's the door bell so I got to run, but I can close this chapter in my life. From this woman's point of view, we're all a work in progress…

The Reality is. . .

As the world marked the 25th anniversary of the first reported case of AIDS, one important story was mostly ignored: AIDS is an epidemic in the African American community and it's spreading fast.

In America today, AIDS is virtually a Black disease, and although many Black leaders and celebrities have embraced the cause of the epidemic's toll in Africa, few have devoted similar energy to the crisis here at home.

Black Americans make up 13 percent of the U.S. population but account for over 50 percent of all new cases of HIV, the virus that causes AIDS. That infection rate is eight times the rate of Whites. Among women, the numbers are even more shocking ~ almost 70 percent of all newly diagnosed HIV-positive women in the United States are Black women. Black women are 23 times more likely to be diagnosed with AIDS than White women, with *heterosexual contact* being the overwhelming method of infection in Black America.

In writing this book, I talked to experts about several key areas that contribute to the spread of AIDS in Black America, including the disproportionate number of Black men in prison. Prisons have AIDS infection rates five times higher than outside the walls, and many men go into prison HIV negative and come out infected, often without knowing it, since there is no mandatory comprehensive national testing, prevention, or treatment program for prison and jail inmates.

Studies conducted on HIV shed light on a complex reality that helps explain why heterosexual transmission among African Americans is so common. Black men are more than twice as likely as White men to have multiple female partners at the same time, statistics show. *Rates of ALL sexually transmitted diseases are higher among African Americans than other groups*, and reality is Black women are the largest casualities of the AIDS war.

And because homosexuality and bisexuality carry such a strong stigma in Black America, African American men may choose to hide their sexual orientation. It's a real problem but nobody wants to talk about it. Even Black churches have been silent on AIDS. My opinion is this, churches in the Black community have an obligation to be "real" about sex and the likelihood of becoming contaminated with this deadly disease. Religious leaders have a social responsibility to society to address, help to prevent, and serve in finding a cure.

Some of it starts with us though. If he wants the kitty bad enough, he will wear a condom. If he really loves you, he won't even question why. He will already know. Hear me when I say that if he walks out of your life because you want to protect yourself ~ then you're better off without him anyway. I hate to be all up in your bedroom, but it's time for us to wake the hell up! Stop playing the victim. Don't even give a second thought to how a man may feel because you have a personal stash of condoms. If you know like I do, you'll have a few in your pursue too.

As women we have to protect ourselves, even when the men we love won't. It's time to start the healing process for Black male-female relationships throughout the world. Where do we start? Let's start by having open dialogue with our mates in regard to monogamous relationships and what *his definition* of monogamy is. Men find it very hard to tell women that they have other sex partners ~ not sure if they fear that they will lose us or if they are more worried that we may be doing the same thing. Whatever it is, if we are to build a sexually safe environment for our children, it starts now by sharing ourselves in a intimate, sensual manner that is not destructive and hazardous to Black society as a whole. *Karma was lucky; you and I may not be...*

Have You Been Tested?

Today, women account for more than one quarter of all new HIV/AIDS diagnoses. Women of color are especially affected by HIV infection and AIDS. In 2004 (the most recent year for which data are available), HIV infection was the leading cause of death for African American women aged 25–34 years.

Of the 126,964 women living with HIV/AIDS, 64% were Black, 19% were White, 15% were Hispanic, 1% were Asian or Pacific Islander, and less than 1% were American Indian or Alaska Native.

Know your status, get tested. For free testing facilities near you visit, www.freeHIVtest.net and tell them Karma sent you…

Until then, love responsibly ~ wear a condom!

I Have!

It Starts Here

Love Responsibly. . .

Spread love today ~ tomorrow is not promised!

You owe it to yourself

Love responsibly. . .

Remember, you are of unmeasurable value

Always pray for me ~ I always do for you. . .

In the Spirit,

Sonya

♥♥♥♥

www.ingramcontent.com/pod-product-compliance
Lightning Source LLC
Chambersburg PA
CBHW050530260626
47157CB00004B/1542